Also by Joseph Rathgeber

The Abridged Autobiography of Yousef R. and Other Stories

MJ

Mixedbloods

Soft Money

Bad Days on the Batsto

Stories

Joseph Rathgeber

Fomite

Burlington VT

"Realpolitik" was previously published with *Green Mountains Review*.

"Parallel Lives" was previously published with *Bull: Men's Fiction*.

ISBN13: 978-1-953236-35-7
Library of Congress Control Number: 2021942172

Fomite
58 Peru Street
Burlington, VT 05401
www.fomitepress.com
11/23/2021

Again and always,
for Michelle,
Joleen, and Cecelia

I began to indulge in the wildest fancies as I lay there in the dark, such as that there was no such town, and even that there was no such state as New Jersey. I fell to repeating the word "Jersey" over and over again, until it became idiotic and meaningless. If you have ever lain awake at night and repeated one word over and over, thousands and millions and hundreds of thousands of millions of times, you know the disturbing mental state you can get into. I got to thinking that there was nobody else in the world but me, and various other wild imaginings of that nature.

—James Thurber

Don't test me, press, or even stress to try to serve me,
'cause I'm down and dirty from the undergrounds of Jersey.

—Tame One

New Jersey was a fresh-mown tomb.

—Sam Lipsyte

Contents

Bad Days on the Batsto — 1

The Noise Demo — 31

Parallel Lives — 41

Evergreen — 50

The Ice Caverns — 59

Sleep Mode — 73

Realpolitik — 92

Super 8 — 100

Mass Surveillance — 117

Ariana Grande — 127

The Bleeding Lodge — 143

A Posthumous Existence — 176

Bad Days on the Batsto

Yes, he was a Black, but I counted Barrel as a friend—hand to God. We all did, it's fair to say. All except Sinclair, who went by Sinny, who—I'll admit if no one else will—had an out-and-out KKK strain to his prejudices. Still, even Sinny shook Barrel's hand when he showed up at our encampment in the Pine Barrens. It was at the invite of a fellow Defender, and so it was all good. Somebody who wouldn't be with us much longer, but somebody who we respected and who had vouched for Barrel, saying the guy had been fed up with food stamp scammers and knew guns. Sounded like a Defender to us, melanin be damned. That's what we were, though: Defenders. It's not something you spoke about openly in Jersey, a blue state teeming with powder puffs. Yes, I'll also say it was a mistake—the invite. We were never anxious to expand our ranks, no. For one, for fear of infiltration. But after we met him, Barrel felt right. He spoke like one of us, and his handshake was firm.

•

We had codenames, which more than one of our wives called childish. But we were of the belief it was pretty cool, not to mention appropriate and called-for. Keeping it cagey, just in case. One of the best was Blood Tax, for example. Goatfucker was another. Explanation behind that one's because of his tattoo of a jihadist fellating one—a goat, I mean. Sinny, I already said. There was Clobber Rob. Bluejean, though he didn't wear denim any more than the rest of us, really. Alex asked to be called Gov Above, but the rhyming bit—consensus agreed—was gaylord, so we just called him Gov. And Barrel, right. But he's no longer "one of us," so to speak. These codenames—there's a hell of a lot of them. Some dudes even changed up midway. Clobber Rob, for some odd reason, used to be Judy. Blood Tax—our de facto leader—he had a list of the codenames in a file on his kid's computer, but he never, despite promises, printed copies for us.

•

Barrel had lost his job late summer—like I had myself. He was let go from his custodial position at a charter school in Newark when they needed extra dough to hire a young, hotshot English teacher who'd published a novel that won a prize. Least that's what Barrel said the Dean of Discipline told him when he was emptying the garbage bin in the admin office the same morning he got shitcanned. I sympathized. I was a career janitor at Roche until the drug-maker unexpectedly closed up shop. Yes, that's right, we were both North Jersey boys, janitors to boot. That made us close as kin in a gaggle of Central and South Jersey Defenders and dumbfucks. Taylor ham, bitches.

•

So that being the history, I had mixed feelings— again, not afraid to admit it—sitting in the makeshift skinning shed with Barrel hogtied across from me, a tear of duct tape across his mouth like a censor bar. He was perspiring so damn much the sweat might've soon freed the adhesive from his face. Raindrops hit the zinc roof, but it may as well had been hail the way it was percussing. I was waiting for someone to update me—instruct me, maybe. I looked at Barrel and thought him asleep, but he might've passed out. His lids were swollen and greased. We called it the skinning shed, but we never actually got around to hunting much. We weren't snipers. We didn't have our act together like *that*.

•

We called ourselves the Crucifix Front even though nearly none of us were Catholics. Gov coined it by the campfire one night. Somewhere along it got shortened to Crux Front, and then the guys took to tatting CRUX on their knuckles and across their backs. We were circulating e-newsletters at one point, and we had /c r u x f r o n t\ stylized in the header like so. We were more excited for that header than the contents of the e-newsletter. Blood Tax kept spelling *quite* wrong. He spelt it *quiet*. I never mentioned to any of the others how much that bothered me. The e-newsletter was an easy way for us to keep up the communicating with one another, but Goatfucker's computer got hacked and we all ended up receiving a bevy of *enlargement* spam and MAKE.MONEY.FAST garbage. That was the end, the discontinuation, the closed coffin on the e-newsletter.

•

Barrel was a shot, man. He tore through the FTX obstacle course. He was more accurate than the rest of us and negotiated turns like a mongoose, irregardless of his heft. We had upright plywood and doors torn off hinges positioned throughout a clearing. Bluejean did home demos so he had gotten the materials, thrown them in the back of his pickup. Barrel studied the course path and racked up direct hits, shredded our silhouettes. Ballistics-wise, Barrel had us beat. Said his daddy was from the Carolinas and taught him on summer vacations down there. The art of aiming and whatnot. His stance was goofy-footed, but nobody questioned it. Nobody can question a guy with that type of precision. On the point of shooting: he took to us, we to him.

•

That first weekend Barrel joined with us, we got to discoursing while Clobber went off at Blood Tax's command to remove the photos we'd tacked up on our targets. They were magazine cover photos, most all of them *Essence* magazines. Clobber Rob had a homeless spell and spent endless hours keeping warm and triple-S-ing in a sink and the handicapped stall at the public library. The librarians threw out back issues by the bundle, and so Clobber grabbed them out of the recycling dumpster. He said he used them to fill his jerkoff coffers. Later, the covers became targets. He ripped them down, successfully, before Barrel could see any black-skinned women in ball gowns.

•

What we looked like was this: fatigues, boonies, and boots. Lawn chairs, camping chairs—any chair that would fold. *In the pines, in the pines.* Like Kurt Cobain sang before he swallowed his shotgun. What we had: AR-15 rifles, 9mm pistols, 5,000 rounds of ammo. "A good start," Blood Tax said. We pitched in for several crossbows and a gun safe. Other funds—monthly collections in one of our hats—went to setting up a makeshift checkpoint on the gravel roadway into our area of the woods. Looksie here: we weren't fucking around. We were defending our way of life. Never put it into writing, but around the campfire we riffed on slogans and such. We sure wasn't anything close to scholars. But together we came up with three mortal enemies—the three G's: gun-grabbers, government, and goatfuckers. So, yes, we ran our drills. We did our due diligence. Chrissake, we had—*have*—children to protect. We weren't sitting around, shooting the shit, shooting shit. This wasn't some coffee klatch. It was serious business.

•

His born name was Darrel. "Darrel" was a short ride to "Barrel." You'd think *gun barrel*, right?—a Bill Cody spinning one. Not so, though. Darrel told us a story about how when he was a kid, he and his brother toppled a pickle barrel in the supermarket. Told us how his mom lost it, gave them whuppings on the spot. Each of them slipping on pickle juice sheeting across the floorspace in front of the deli counter. He had us in stitches the way he told it. Won a lot of us over with that tale. And afterwards, naturally, "Barrel" was born.

•

We slogged through dark swamps in boots. Followed the waterways. Blood Tax argued you never knew when you might need to take to rougher terrain. Only a handful of us had waders. The white cedars bent over riverbanks like gran-gran's arthritic fingers. Barrel called the white cedars *false-cypress*, and so, retrospectively, that should've been a sign we weren't on the same page.

•

Trust was topmost. For some of us, with Barrel, it came on slow. Sinny and Goatfucker, 'specially. I once came back from a long, damp weekend in early November—that's when FTX got *really* real—and tried to tell my ex about it, how Sinny and Goat had been going at Barrel, but she dismissed it. She never wanted to talk about the group, waved it away. I'd try to preach to her a bit—talk about being anti-gov and what that meant, talk about confiscation, naturally—but she wanted none of it. She made it a habit to laugh off our numbers, our ranks. We had manpower enough, though. And firepower aplenty. Trust me on that. I once told her about Bluejean's short-wave and she made this face I could've crushed and said, *Aww, ain't that cute!*

•

Sinny took to calling Barrel "Rodney." *Rodney, fetch that water jug now.* Or, speaking of the silhouette targets, *Go re-set that, Rodney. Rodney, pass the mayo. Save some for the fish, Rodney*, as Barrel chugged a Michelob Ultra the same as the rest of us. Do this, *Rodney*. Do that, *Rodney*. Ordering him around. Sinny was relentless with it. Sinny saw the world through a scope, and Barrel seemed to always be in the crosshairs.

•

The number of months Barrel was with us, by my estimate, had to be around nine. He appeared somewhere-abouts in October and ended up in knotted ropes on the floor of the skinning shed in late June. Earlier that month it grew unseasonably hot. We bemoaned the humidity, and Blood Tax actually gave a little and cut exercises short. The lot of us ran like schoolgirls into the Batsto River for a skinny dip. Wasn't all fun-and-games, though. That was how we bathed in the summer out there. It was that or ragging down out of metal buckets. I liked the feel of my feet in the Batsto—the river mud's enriched with bog ore. I liked to think of iron between my toes. Hand to God, that always got me going, made me think big picture.

So this one time when we were in there, soaping ourselves and sunning, all eyes fell on Barrel. It was the first time he'd washed like this with us, and his body was something else. He had leper-like razor bumps in a strip along his neckline. Said he couldn't keep them away. He'd taken to pressing tea bags to the area. *Tannic acid*, he said. Sure as hell wasn't doing the job, though. And his chest—straight on down his sternum, heading southward—was scarred like the whittle wood my uncle is always hacking at. Gov said the scar looked like the landmasses on the globe in his granddaddy's study.

It was a burn, Barrel said. Told us how when he was young his fam never had hot water enough to fill a tub. *Poor and black*—that old racket. So instead of sitting in ice water, his mother taught him early on how to boil a big, black stockpot on the stove by himself. He'd hold the handles with dishrags and hobble the heavy stockpot across the kitchen and into the bathroom to pour into the tub. It was a daring feat, and he had to hold the pot steady so as not to splash. Keeping in mind Barrel was a small boy at the time, and that pot practically matched him in height. But it was worth it to temper the bathwater to where it needed to be—not nearly lukewarm, but not so cold it caused hypothermia.

But, as you could surmise, one fine, dingy day in a tenement in Newark, little Barrel went about boiling the water and—he claims—tripped on his own shoelace. The stockpot spilled over—not outward, but inward—and sizzled down his bony chest. Barrel was laid out on the linoleum floor for a solid two hours with only his younger brother kneeling over him gently pressing dishrags to the wound. Latchkey kids both, the littler one cried and cried when their mother finally got home from work.

•

On the following Saturday, hot still, getting fresh and clean in the Batsto again, Clobber Rob commented on another aspect of Barrel's anatomy. Clobber was a survivalist in the strictest sense. He had the canned goods to prove it. Slept with a .38 under his pillow and his flint hooked through his belt loop. His hair was hay-straight and had the uneven lengths and slants of a man who cuts it himself in a mirror with black moisture spots. Yeah, it was *that* bad. Clobber swirled his hand at the surface of the water to get our attention and called out, "Look at the cottonmouth on *him!*" And Sinny answered back, "I ain't messin' with that pit viper. No way, no how!"

•

At night we'd get all kumbaya around the campfire. There was this shredded tarp in the tree above where we sat. We sat in a circle, like a coven. We didn't have any cauldron, though—a baked bean can on the fire was all.

But I'd sip my Ultra and spread my legs, dig my heels into the dirt, and tilt my head back at the night sky. Instead of stars, though, I'd just look at that tarp the wind had whipped up into the branches one weekend. It tangled and got tore up. Its blue was a striking contrast to the dark. It got so goddamn ratty and beard-like. I couldn't see no constellations but for what appeared in the torn microfibers of that tarp.

•

We would swap stories. Clobber Rob—still back when he was Judy—talked about why he'd been so late in arriving at the encampment. "You're amateur-hour-ing it," Blood Tax had said, giving him shit frontways and sideways. "I got stuck," Clobber Rob explained, "in a funeral procession on the Parkway. Must've been somebody important—a politician or something. Police escorts. Those attachable black and white funeral flags were flapping on each and every car going on for what had to be close to a mile. I couldn't get through or around it. Hell, I got absorbed *into* it."

Barrel had an answer for that one. "I got T-boned once while in a funeral procession, if you'll believe it. We were just on local streets in the Ironbound and had come to an intersection. And there's always that hesitation somewhere in the long line of cars when the light turns red. Nobody ever knows if the funeral privilege means you can run it. Well, light turned red and I went for it. Just as some junker driven by an old, overeager man laid onto his gas pedal and plowed right into me. I mean, he had the green, but you gotta be aware, ya'know? And this old man, he died. There I was in a funeral procession, then I was getting T-boned, and the man doing the damage dies on the scene. It was just piling death on death. Like a mass grave."

Clobber leaned over to me—his mouth behind his mustache and his Michelob—and muttered: *I call bullshit.*

•

"It cakes and is a bitch to get off," Bluejean said. "I can't be bothered about it." We were talking about the windshield on his Isuzu. It had gotten mud-splattered on the drive in and there was no way in heaven or hell he could see out of it. "I just duck down low or raise up high," was how he described the negotiations he made on the fly. Blood Tax—in his infinite and all-knowing wisdom—went on and on about washing windshields with newspaper pages. Far gone drunk, most of us weren't fighting him much on the point. But he kept asserting it as though we had something significant to gain by it. "No streaks," he said. "Not a one."

•

Goatfucker staggered into our campfire circle—his dick still dripping piss and hanging from his zipper—rapping:

I own the Camaro and the mobile home, so where the fuck you gonna go? He fell into his lawn chair like a ton of bricks. Almost broke through the webbing.

"Would you go further beyond the perimeter to do that, please?" Blood Tax said to him.

Goatfucker bowed his head. "The forest is my john, Mr. Tax." He said it in a regal way. His eyes were all but shut, narrow slits of pink. "Or do you prefer *Mr. Blood?*"

"I prefer somebody serve us up some grub." Clobber Rob removed a three-pound Taylor ham from an ACME plastic bag. "Get on at it now!" Blood Tax encouraged.

So Clobber started hacking at the butt of the Taylor ham with a bowie knife, freeing the salty meat from its cotton sheath.

"You sprung for the family-size pork roll, I see," Gov Above commented.

"Pork roll?" Barrel said. "That's Taylor ham."

"Like hell," Sinny said.

"I second that," I said, speaking up to defend Barrel on the name.

"And I said *like hell,*" Sinny yelled now. "Fuck North Jersey motherfuckers know about anything?"

Clobber stopped slicing.

"Chill the fuck out, will you?" Blood Tax said. He waved at Clobber. "You! Keep slicing!"

The slices were piled and systematically spread around a large skillet. Heavy-duty, cast iron one. Clobber put three cuts on the outer edge of each slice.

"Don't let 'em bubble," Bluejean said, his mouth full of beer.

"You see me cutting?" Clobber said. He pointed the bowie knife at Bluejean's chest. It would've been threatening if the two of them hadn't known each other since Eagle Scouts.

"Make yourself useful and pass out the hard rolls." That was Blood Tax to Bluejean.

Sinny raised up off his chair and pissed against a tree well within the perimeter Blood Tax had just requested Goatfucker go beyond. He whistled while he yellowed the ground. We could see the foaminess of it shimmering in the moonlight at the tree roots. Sinny let his head bobble and then shouted back at the group over his shoulder, his manhood still in his hands.

"You know what, Blood? You being bossy as fuck this weekend."

Blood Tax shook his head. The meat sizzled in the skillet. Clobber moved the slices around in their own grease, flipping them when the edges got charred.

"Pork roll…Taylor ham…" Sinny was approaching the campfire again. "These things matter!" He plopped down in his chair and clapped his big-ass hands a bunch of times, aggressively like. "*These, things, matter,* my friends. What you call shit. How you name it. All that adds up. We're talking about culture here, aren't we? Isn't food culture? So," he ended his soliloquy with an effeminate flair, a flick of the wrist, "it *matters.*"

"What matters most," I said, defusing, "is who's got the ketchup?"

We made our sandwiches—meager meals always being the best. Just salted meat slapped onto a hard roll, ketchup squirt, donezo. We chowed, and every-body shut the fuck up for a few minutes. But then—I should've figured it would go like this—Sinny started in on Barrel again.

"How old are you, Rodney?"

Barrel's slow chewing and lifeless eyes let me know he wasn't too keen on the "Rodney" racket again. "Y'all don't crack, right? So it's hard for me to tell, is all."

Barrel, as if hoping to shut Sinny up, told him.

Sinny perked, calculated on his fingers, and shot a look over at Goatfucker. I'd never seen Sinny so goddamn giddy.

"Shit, you was born in '88?" he asked Barrel.

"What of it?" Barrel poked a loose triangle of Taylor ham into his mouth.

Sinny looked to Goatfucker again, kind of smiling sneakily, as if they were sharing in the knowledge of something.

"Oh, nothing, nothing," he answered. "That's just a number I like. One I'm partial to."

Barrel was oblivious to all the neo-Nazi nudging they were doing. It was better off that way, I thought.

•

That same night I drove out of the woods for a beer run and asked Barrel to come with. He did, and we took his car—a Civic with three rims.

"Your car don't match you," I told him.

We arrived out of the pitch darkness of the woods at the roadway. We still had a maze of dirt roads before we hit any asphalt, though.

"Same car I had since high school," he said. "I used to trick it out. Me and my brother were into it—always reading car mags and shit."

"What's with the fourth rim?"

"Shit, man," he said. "With the kid there's no chance in hell of getting that last one."

Barrel hadn't ever spoke about his kid before, not to the group at large, anyways. Not to me.

"You got a boy or a girl?"

"Girl."

"Hey, man. Me too. How old?"

He leaned forward in his seat, stretching his seatbelt like the Kevlar bowstring on a compound, and stared at my chest.

"She's six," he said, and then he pointed at me, or beyond me—it was actually more at the roof of the car. "Can you buckle your seatbelt? We're on the road now."

I did it just 'cause. He was off, frazzled or something. I think Sinny had gotten to him.

"I got a daughter, too," I said. "She's about the same. Seven—eight in October, though."

"Oh yeah?"

"Yeah. She's a good kid. Smart as a whip in school."

"Mine, too," he said, but not in a competitive way. Not like we was comparing. Just stating it. Two men talking. That's what it was.

We were silent for most of the ride, neither of us with much to say. But it wasn't terribly awkward either. It just was. When we pulled into the parking lot, I patted the dash and told him to hang tight. *I got this*, is what I said to him—meaning both paying for the cases of Michelob Ultra and the going into the liquor store and getting it. When I came back and squeezed the cases into the backseat (I saw a booster back there— same brand my ex has for our daughter), I tried to make a joke to start things right again. Keep the conversation going. Barrel cut me off, though.

"What the fuck's Sinny's problem? Goatfucker, too."

"What do you mean?" I said, dumbly.

Barrel pulled off down the road. I heard the cases shift in the backseat, so I turned around and adjusted them, secured them better. When I turned frontwards again, I buckled my seatbelt and said *I don't know.*

"They got a grudge or something."

"Well, hold on," I said. "Now you talking 'they.' Who's 'they'?"

"Sinny and Goatfucker, mostly."

"Those two go at everybody," I told him. He wasn't buying it, though. I just kept on making the case. I told him, I said, "Hand to God, Barrel, the guy's are cool with you. We got a brotherhood out here, a fraternity." *Hand to God*, I said, but fingers crossed. I knew I was being mendacious as a mofo. But what was I gonna tell him?

"Point blank," he said. "I think they got issues with my being Black."

"Nah, nah, nah," I told him. I was waving my hands in front of me like I was working to wipe away the darkness ahead of us. "It ain't like that, Barrel. It's not. You know, I even know for a fact that Goatfucker's got a brother that dates a Black girl. And him, man, and Sinny, they don't mean nothing by it with that Rodney business. For real. They're just joshing you. Getting your goat. So you just got to make sure you don't let it get got."

I couldn't tell you if I was making headway with him or if he was just done hearing me talk. But he dropped it. We drove on, and I kept thinking about that one rear tire without the rim.

Reception was awful out there on the encampment, and Blood Tax pooh-poohed us using technology beyond the barest of the bare anyway. But I checked my cell and read a message from my ex. It was something about how our daughter was flipping out, refusing to go to sleep, and how she had just about had enough of it. The message was a big block of text. She took aim at me for being at the encampment that weekend, which was supposed to be my weekend with the kid. I relayed this all to Barrel in the hopes of stirring up some conversation.

"Bedtime has always been an issue with Julie—our daughter."

Barrel nodded.

"I mean, she used to put us through the wringer. Nothing was easy. Getting her undressed, bath time, getting her pajamas. All her stuffed animals had to be set about a particular way in her crib—it was crazy."

"Mine's like that, too," Barrel said, finally giving something up.

"Yeah, I mean—for fuck's sake. She would refuse to brush her teeth and we'd have to all but beg her to open wide. I'd have the top row done and then she'd bite down on the brush and not let go. She'd clamp down for dear life. It was a circus."

"You know what, Kathleen—my girl—she kills us with the teeth, too."

"Why're they so difficult with the teeth, right?"

There was rhythm to what we were saying now. We were commiserating and chuckling like two old friends catching up. There was a looseness to it. Barrel—who had, up to that point, been wound up tighter than virgin asshole—slouched down in the driver's seat and gave his seatbelt a bit of slack.

"You know what else?" he said. "Just last week— Kat's losing her teeth now. Left and right. Seems like another one's loose every other day. Well, last week, she accidentally swallowed one." He made a gulping sound, motion. "Right down the gullet. She freaked the fuck out. I felt bad for her. She really was scared about it. And then, of course, shit got even more intense when she thought, for a second, she wouldn't get any Tooth Fairy money out of the deal without the hard proof."

"Hey, man. Julie did the same thing. She was eating corn on the cob and it went right down the pipe. Couldn't tell kernel from tooth. She was devastated, too."

Most everyone had passed out by the time we got back to the encampment, notably Sinny and Goatfucker. Barrel helped me haul the Michelob Ultra cases, and, when we had finished the job, I patted him on the back. Small gestures, right?

Fast-forward a couple hours later—dead of night, now—and we're all nearly stricken with heart attacks at the sudden shouting of shots popping off. We rush from our tents, most shirtless and squinty-eyed, with weapons at the ready. And what we see is Barrel firing off rounds, eating away at tree trunks until the whole scene is sap splattered.

This was a man possessed, I tell you. He was out there—as awake as a raccoon—goofy-footed and taking out targets without flinching. Blood Tax finally got a word in as he went to reload. First he got him to stop— snapped him out of whatever reverie he was in. Then reprimanded him, like. No matter how remote we are, you can't fire off like that at night, he told him.

Thinking I could build off whatever we'd shared earlier, I took Barrel aside and told him the same. He was in a zone, though. Somewhere else. Some*body* else, too.

"I couldn't sleep," he said. "I get nightmares."

"Hell," I said. "I do, too. We all do. All of America does, for Chrissakes. But you got to find some other way of getting them gone. This," I said firm as was needed, "can't be the way."

•

And then this went and happened the following week.

Barrel took it upon himself to invite his kid brother to the encampment. Didn't run it by a soul. He was out of line and not at all apologetic about it. So, I mean, what did he expect would happen?

His brother wasn't him, that's for sure. Trey or Jay or something was his name. I don't remember it clearly—not remembering much about those 24-to-36 hours clearly. But if you bring in an outsider like that—we don't care if it's mother, father, sister, brother, black, white, up, or down—we, as a group, gonna have much to say about it. We're gonna give a lot of lip to it. A lot of cold-shouldering. And we did.

Some guys went at Barrel's brother harder than others. Antagonized, sure. But, as I said, you can't just be rolling up with plus-ones to a covert encampment in the woods. Can't happen.

•

Barrel's brother's vision was so bad, apparently, the lenses in his glasses so thick, that his head looked narrow as fuck when you spoke to him straight on. And we each took turns looking at him that way, sizing him up around the campfire. All outlaw activities had come to a screeching halt when Barrel arrived with him, and so we really had nothing else to do but grill him. You can guess who the main instigators were.

Sinny and Goatfucker sat side-by-side. They elbowed each other, egging each other on. Goat started in on the dude's ball cap. Asked him about it.

"My fitted?" Barrel's brother asked.

"No," Goat said, "your ball cap."

He spoke at him like you speak to a busboy or a cleaning lady that don't speak a lick of English. Goat asked why he still had the sticker on the bill, which was a hologram. It shimmered when it caught the firelight.

"It keeps it fresh, ya' know?" is what Trey/Jay answered.

"No," Goat said, "I don't know. Fresh? What? You wearing a fucking vegetable on your head?"

To this, Sinny laughed like it was the granddaddy of all jokes.

I entertained the thought of coming to Barrel's defense. Telling Sinny and Goat to let it be. But I didn't. I didn't because Barrel brought this upon himself. It was indefensible. And, if I did speak up, it wouldn't be defending Barrel even. It would be defending his brother, who I didn't know from Adam.

Everyone seemed to be taking it all in—this ruthless heckling being carried out by Goatfucker. They all slugged back Ultras and patted their bellies. They took turns pissing beyond Blood Tax's perimeter. Blood Tax, for his part, seemed to have abdicated his power position. He crossed his legs like a woman and watched as Sinny and Goat went hard at Barrel's brother. I detected a strong *Do what you will* vibe from him.

"How come you don't bend the bill?" Sinny asked, taking the reins from Goat.

"Just how I wear it."

Barrel's bro was holding the same unopened beer can in his hands since he sat.

"Just how you wear it, yo. Shit," Sinny nudged Goat, "we used to bend the bill around a baseball and rubber band it over night. We wouldn't be caught dead with a flat bill. We'd be made fools of for that sort of faggotry."

"That's right." Goat had this constant nod going on. His eyes were closed. Sinny's were fixed on his target.

"Damn fools, for sure. If you came out of the house with your ball cap too big for your own damn head, sticker still on it, bill flat as fuck—well, let's say you'd be looking for some unwanted attention. You know what I mean, yo?"

Barrel's brother—I think it was Jay, now that I've considered it—looked at Barrel. Little brother looking at big brother for guidance sort of look. Barrel shook his head, like, *Let it go. Ignore. Do nothing. I'll take you home soon as I finish this beer.*

"What's with the *yo*?" Jay asked.

"Come again, Rodney?"

Here I leaned forward. I might've said *Cool it* to Sinny, but I might've not.

"Why you keep saying *yo* like that, like you're trying to mock me?"

"Ooh, ooh, ooh," Sinny started up. "Listen…"

"Need to watch what you say now, Rodney," Goat jumped in.

"Fuck that, man!" Jay said. And he said it with such emphasis that near everyone at the campfire lunged forward to check him.

Barrel put his arm across his little brother's chest. It was like that reflex you do in the car when you got your girl sitting shotgun and you stop short. How you think the skin and muscle and bone of your arm's gonna be enough to keep her from flying through the windshield.

Blood Tax, finally, spoke up. Our voice of reason. Our levelheaded leader. Our cooler head prevailing. Or so I thought before he came out with this:

"Alright now, alright now. Listen," and he looked Jay dead in the eyes, "us people of color got to stick together."

Jay curled his lip in a way that changed his face completely—and pointed across the fire at Blood Tax as if to say, *Did this guy really just say that?*

Bluejean got up to piss. Gov gathered empties in a trash bag. Goatfucker disappeared behind the open door of his pickup, ostensibly to lean in and get at the cigarette lighter for a smoke. I didn't know where in the world Clobber Rob went off to. Blood Tax glared at Jay. And Sinny stayed seated, seeming swami-like. There was an aura around him, manic and maddening energies swirling about his sweaty head.

I, for my part, slumped down in my lawn chair and stared at the constellations in the shredded, blue tarp up above in the trees. I did that, and I sipped nervously on my seventh Ultra, feeling the alcohol and feeling the intensity of the moment. I want to say, though, through it all I stayed by Barrel's side.

"You see these freckles under my eyes?" Jay asked. He pointed and poked at the area. Sure enough, he was freckled. It wasn't something that needed attention brought to it.

"These freckles, you see them?" he asked again. He was asking it of Blood Tax, mainly. "I got these because your ancestors raped mine."

Blood Tax smirked and Sinny shifted. His head moved in a way that I only later realized was a signal, a *Now.*

Barrel was pushed and fell from his chair and collapsed onto me. His beer splashed against my beard and down the center of my shirt. I heard the jangly thud of Goatfucker swinging a tube sock filled with Parkway tokens against Jay's skull. His pristine ball cap fell to the ground like a piece of merchandise off a store shelf.

It was a commotion, but there was very little being said. It was as though the Pine Barrens smothered any sounds that might've come out of our insignificant encampment in the woods. I struggled to gather myself as Sinny and Blood Tax took a hold of Barrel, drunk and helpless in any attempt to protect his brother. So we both watched—Barrel and myself—as the rest of the guys beat little brother to a pulp—Clobber with a gun butt, the others with their fists and oak firewood.

•

They threw his body in the Batsto.

I wasn't there to see it. I was put on Barrel duty. Sinny and Blood Tax restrained him, Blood whistled, and Clobber came through with nylon rope and bungee cords and hogtied Barrel up good. Sinny took an almost sensual pleasure in placing the duct tape across Barrel's mouth. He kept smiling, saying *yeah, yeah, yeah.*

They shut me up in the skinning shed with Barrel. Sinny gave him a few swift blows to the gut and he was floored. *Hold tight*, Blood Tax said—to me, not Barrel. So I did.

•

It was late and I was well and drunk, so my grip on time got all screwy in the skinning shed. They were gone for what seemed forever, doing and dealing with Barrel's brother whatever, and however, they were.

What they did was throw Jay's body in the Batsto and, I later learned, decided they would figure what to do with it the morning after. Rainfall started serious, and—though they had left the body half-in-the-river, half-on-the-bank—the level rose and nearly submerged the body. They had no idea how bloated he'd be.

•

I felt forgotten. My mind zigzagged trying to follow the pattern of the raindrops on the zinc roof. Barrel got so still. He was on the floor, no more than three feet from me. I sat in one corner and he was like a piece of furniture—an ottoman, maybe—in another. He was a heap. So silent, too. Not even a grunt out of him.

Trying to rewind and remember all that had happened, what had transpired to get me where I was, I couldn't cobble it together. It all happened. This is weird, but—hand to God—it was like the night I lost my virginity. How one event led into the next and the results occurred, I couldn't tell you. It's not a coherent thing. Like I said, it all just *happened*.

I began to think about possibilities. Like, say I went all renegade and cut Barrel free. Fact is, I didn't sign up—no way, no how—for any killing or kidnapping or nothing, not in this way. In that skinning shed, I got real hung up on brethren and objectives and what the hell we were really doing in them woods. I thought I knew.

I could escape him. Things were quiet enough. I didn't hear any voices. Knowing every one of those guys, not a one of them would want to miss out on the action down at the Batsto. That meant I could untie Barrel, get him to his Civic, lug his beaten body into the passenger seat, and drive toward the main road. I could get him home. That's what I started thinking on—*I could get him home.* I could send him back to his daughter with the baby tooth in her belly. And I could get home to my daughter, too. And I could find another group of likeminded guys. Maybe over the border in PA— plenty there. I could get back to my place. I could take a hot shower. I'd have to fiddle and fight and fuck with the diverter on the tub spout that always sticks, but I could get it. I'd get it eventually. And then the water'd be running out of the showerhead. It'd be running hot. The water would roll over my body—down my head, my shoulders, all the way down my back. And, sure, the clogged drain would make it so my feet were sub-merged in inches of water made filthy by the soil of my own body, but it wouldn't be the raindrops percussing off the zinc roof. No, it wouldn't be that. It would be something so far removed from the encampment, from the rest of the guys standing bankside at the Batsto, racking their brains about what to do about that damn black body in the Pine Barrens. I'd be living anony-mously in the density of North Jersey, safe and sound and showered. I could fill the bathroom with steam. I could shower until the water ran cold and then shut off the fixture. I could obscure the reflection in the mirror. I could stare at the mirror and not even see myself. I could do all that, I could.

I heard boots getting closer in the mud—the way the soles of them sucked at the mud with each step. The door on the skinning shed pushed open, and Sinny walked in. He looked to me and said, "'Nough fucking around in here. What we gonna do with this one?"

The Noise Demo

CURT WAS RIDING BITCH on the way to the noise demo, but nobody in the car called it that.

"Make a left at the light, and then go straight," Taylor said.

His older sister, who was sitting shotgun, gave directions to the driver—a greased over guy of origins unknown with a ski mask rolled up along his forehead.

"Forward," Nicole said.

Nicole was sitting to the right of Curt. She was his sister's best friend since tee-ball, and he was trying to lose himself in the side-by-side rub of their bodies. He sniffed her hair when she leaned in to correct Taylor and was disappointed that she didn't smell like her, but like patchouli and tent funk. Like Taylor, she'd sworn off Ban roll-ons for reasons Curt had grown tired of understanding.

Everyone in the Mazda was dressed like cat burglars, including Curt. His black jeans were tucked into his black tube socks, which were snugged into his laced-up Docs. He had black leather gloves, a black pea coat, and he was topped off with a black skully.

"My parents deadnamed me three times this weekend," Taylor said to Nicole.

Nicole said, "Are you fucking serious?"

Taylor had moved out. She was supposedly living with Nicole in an apartment across town, but she never gave her parents a mailing address or anything. Curt had his suspicions she was living somewhere else but no hard proof. Taylor talked a lot about squatter's rights.

She came home on weekends to do laundry for a few hours. She'd sit at the kitchen table flicking her phone and not welcoming conversation from anyone. Curt didn't remember her making an issue of what their parents called her. They did have it out over the detergent, though. The fact that their dad hadn't gotten the fragrance free one.

"This your first demo?" the driver asked.

"We've dragged him to a few marches in the city," Taylor said. "Didn't we bring you to Bluestockings for a meeting last summer?"

"I think so," he said.

"That's so rad," the driver said.

Curt said, "Yeah."

He couldn't see the driver's hands. He held the wheel at six and seven. From the backseat, it looked like he was steering with his hands in his lap. Curt counted the red and white marker balls on the power lines as they drove down the highway. They were moving slowly in the right lane. Curt's dad taught him when he was still in a booster seat that driving slow on the highway is more dangerous than driving fast. He thought about how the driver would be primed for a launch through the windshield based off the position of his hands.

Curt's sister's hands were raw. She picked at her cuticles and gnawed off the skin around the nails. He saw it when she reached her hands back on the headrest to hold Nicole's.

"You've read Gelderloos, haven't you?" the driver asked Curt. His eyes were like a raccoon's in the rearview, glowing.

"Nah," Curt said. "I don't think so."

"What about Bob Black?"

"Hmm," Curt paused, "no, I don't think I've read his stuff yet. Maybe a little."

"Aragorn?"

"I haven't had much time for reading," Curt tried.

"Oh, man!" the driver turned his body to look at Curt eye-to-eye. "He's *essential*. I'll get you a copy. I've got some printouts of his shit."

"My brother barely reads his name," Taylor said. "I gave him my copy of *The Conquest of Bread* and he didn't even open it."

Curt had opened it. He found it full of post-its and scribblings in the margins, which was saying a lot, since the margins were so narrow. He could never read a book with that many words on a page.

"I read it," he said. "She doesn't know what I read." He scrunched his face at his sister.

"What'd you think, though?"

"Very dense," Curt told the driver, which is what he'd heard others say more than once about books.

"My nav says take this exit," Nicole said. They were getting close to the prison. It was nearly midnight and Taylor cracked her window for a cigarette. Curt's chapped lips stung at the feel of the brick air.

"Could you not?" he said.

"I just need a drag," Taylor said.

Nicole told her, "Me too."

Taylor passed the cigarette to Nicole. Curt didn't mind that so much. He liked how the Parliament fit between her straightened fingers. It looked like she was blowing him a kiss, but all that came out was smoke.

"I read *Motorcycle Diaries*," he said, leaning forward onto the console.

"That's pretty rad," the driver said. "Kinda dated, but good."

They had to walk some ways to get to the prison gate. It wasn't what Curt expected. The prison was fortified, but not garishly. It could've been any factory. He half-expected to see phalanxes of cops in riot gear guarding the place, but there was none of that. The gate was closed and locked with mechanisms beyond their daring, and the pigs were, presumably, watching them on the security cameras, safe and warm inside, sipping dreggy coffee from a trough.

The driver had pulled down his ski mask and carried a Rubbermaid tote in his arms, not gracefully.

"What's in the box?" Curt asked.

"Explosives," Nicole told him, shouldering in close to him, interrupting his stride.

"Fireworks," Taylor said. "We're gonna set them off."

Curt said, "Fourth of July comes early this year," which he thought pretty clever, but his sister ended him.

"Fuck the Fourth of July," she said. "It's a crock of shit! You should know that, if I've taught you anything. Frederick Douglass. Read him on the subject and then come talk to me, Curtis."

"I thought he didn't read," the driver said, a lippy smile pushing through the mouth hole on his mask.

"Shut up, Jad," Taylor said.

Curt committed the driver's name to memory. Jad, for whom all things were rad.

When they gathered in the meeting spot with everyone else who'd made the drive down to the prison, the mood was joyful, even in the shadow of concertina wire. Curt wandered the crowd, his hands dug in his pockets for warmth. He watched someone drag a folding table out of their station wagon and set up necessary items: sloppily stapled zines, flyers for upcoming actions, and noisemakers for those who didn't bring their own. Curt picked up a whistle and examined it like a bone.

"You want some hot cocoa?" a girl with dreads asked him. "It's cold, right?"

"Yeah," he said, put off by her politeness.

"Go over to the passenger side door. Henry's got the pot."

She whistled to Henry and Henry waved Curt over.

"Here," he said, and he shoved a paper cup of Swiss Miss at him. It even had the mini marshmallows.

"You ready?" Henry asked him.

Curt burnt his top lip on the cocoa.

"Ready for what?"

"To let the comrades on the inside know they're not forgotten, man."

"Oh, yeah," Curt said. He turned around and looked off at the prison again. It was monolithic and its grays matched the clouds in the night sky.

He didn't know what else to say, but Henry was standing there as though a conversation was owed.

"Have you read Gelderloos?"

"Shit yeah," Henry said. "Who hasn't?"

Two women with red bandanas tied around their wrists ladder-carried a sign that read PRISONS ARE OBSOLETE in Christmas lights on a slab of cardboard and plugged into a portable power box.

Curt tried to find Taylor and Nicole but couldn't. He settled in with a group of people wearing matching gray gaiters. One of them was sitting on a cajón, drumming a simple beat that got Curt's head nodding. Others joined in with claps, muffled by fleece and Carhartt cowhide gloves.

A call-and-response started up, and Curt shouted the slogans right along. Not only did it make him feel significantly more included than Taylor and Nicole did, but it warmed him up. Heat seemed to radiate through his layers of clothing and swell his bones. They'd explode at the onset of the revolution.

He heard the high-frequency squeal of fireworks shooting into the sky. They soared over the fence and illuminated the prison walls, casting shadows in deranged ways. Dazzling, sparkling lights lit up the cold night, and it was so strange that it came from such a morosely outfitted mass of people.

Jad must be nearby, he thought, and Taylor and Nicole with him. He could follow the trajectory of the aerials back to where they were. He could rejoin his sister as she crouched to light the wicks snaking from the mortars. But then explosions started happening simultaneously, shooting off from other corners of the crowd. He gave up on the search and stared up at the show.

The guy on the cajón was beating it wildly, channeling some cosmic or celestial higher level. It was like he was conjuring a conduit to Milford Graves. One thing Curt knew better than his sister and her friends was music. Fuck those books she flaunted. He had the universal truth and soul force of his music collection.

Curt shouted until his lungs burned and the corners of his mouth slit. Sparklers ignited all around him, with people winding the wires through the air like wands. Roman candles popped off, air horns blared, and ratchets made the mechanical noise of manufactured chaos. Curt put the whistle to his mouth and blew a sporadic and holy sound.

It was a cacophony of screams—of jubilation and ironclad agony. Curt felt his body swell with vibrations.

He thought of the Fourth of July, against his sister's admittedly better judgment, and how the sky looks after the fireworks show ends and there's just smoke in senseless shapes drifting down and away. That's the end of summer, he thought, right then. Everything from Independence Day on is humid and overgrown gardens and skunks lurking the streets freely. Next thing you know it's the end of summer blues, truly. The last week in August before school starts is a sad death, an assisted suicide with a plastic bag, drawstring, and can of helium. Then it's the decay of autumn, the white of winter, misery, et cetera.

But the smoke wasn't drifting yet. The crowd's stockpile of explosives seemed bottomless. The cops still hadn't showed up. There were no showdowns. No pipe-bombs or Molotovs. The fountains of pretty fire kept on. How materials so destructive and dangerous could usher in such beauty, now that was something to write a book about.

Curt heard the crowd's erratic patterns of noise crescendo—a rise so sudden he at first thought the demo had turned deadly. People pointed, and he saw lights flicker on and off in cell windows up and down the many broad faces of the prison. The comrades on the inside could hear the ruckus, and they knew they weren't forgotten. And in that same moment Curt remembered why he was becoming who he was determined to become.

Parallel Lives

Sometimes he thinks he's living parallel lives.

He was reading about some kid, I'm sure, no younger than himself, who had died in a cave—what do they call it—*spelunking?* One local news channel reported that, while another said he and his friends were only exploring it. They just went in and never came out. Not until they came out as shrouded cadavers.

This is the thing with my husband and the internet. Staring at a screen keeps him awake, the whites of his eyes bloodying gradually, but he goes down these black holes and can't keep from looking. He tells me there's the possibility of finding something transcendent there.

This cave kid, he learned, documented freight train

graffiti. He did a lot of *benching*, that is, he sat on a bench and waited for trains to pass. Hubby bemoans corporations when we have people over, but he drools over even the idea of seeing "BNSF" or "CSX" bold and big on the sides of those gondolas. As though inter-modal transport isn't corporate. Hubby found out the kid hopped freights, too—didn't just look at them. He "rode the blinds," like they sing about in those crackling blues songs he loves so dearly.

So Hubby was reading about all this: blues, benching, and death by cave. Hyperlink after hyperlink after hyperlink. He was darkening them all. His eyes, I'll bet, were bloodshot, but his chest just welled up like never before. And this is why I say parallel lives. Because he's too much of a punk coward to commit to anything like that. He feels compelled to do it but can't. He's scared to death of the cave death, all that pitch darkness and chthonic swallowing up. Gulp.

I am a cave kid, he tells himself. *Cave kid is me.* As if to convince himself.

And this mantra-ing is interrupted, and therefore ends, as I call him to say I'm on my way home from the urologist. I call him to cry, to bawl like the severest orgasm he's ever heard me heave. Because I've been brutalized, and I can't help but tell him about it. Silent suffering isn't for me, not here.

I don't tell about it in full, though, not until hours later—home, children tucked, tea steeping.

"I don't know how a UTI ended me up in this situation," I tell him.

"What happened?" he presses. "Tell me exactly what happened."

I tell him exactly what happened: piss in a cup (that warm, dark yellow from being held); a bladder scan; a catheter (that is, a brutalization).

"That's not exact," he says. And he's right.

The bladder scan because they wanted to check my postvoid residual volume. "The leftover pee in my bladder," I tell him. The catheter because the scan showed my bladder was still full—a reading which defied the logic of my insides. The quintessence of this botched examination was the catheter, though.

"The nurse had me lie back on the table and spread my legs. She told me it wouldn't hurt, no more than inserting a tampon. But she had me moving up and down the table. 'Move closer,' she said. 'Back up now.' And she was just jabbing at me with that tube, excruciatingly, trying to find pee? 'This isn't right,' she kept saying. 'This is so strange.' She forgot I was there. Forgot there was embodiment around that urethra. This was no tampon, trust me. Turned out my bladder was empty. I heard her in the hall, the bladder scan machine and its wires gathered in her arms like a garden harvest of fresh-picked vegetables, tell another nurse, 'I told you this machine isn't working right.' I heard her say that. I was zipping my jeans back on."

I tell him this but not like this. I'm not this articulate or structured. I'm crying, bawling. Hubby holds me, rubbing my upper arms, shoulders, and back. He's putting me back together. He's trying to make me, all my parts, me again. Wholly, fully, functionally me. It doesn't work. I don't tell him it doesn't work because I feel it would be the wrong thing to say, to say that it doesn't work. It would be like calling into question his ability to effectually love.

I look over Hubby's shoulder—his hands and arms still doing that rubbing; he's trying to erode me to a mental state more manageable. More befitting a marriage. It's as if he believes friction will free me of my trauma.

Out the window I see a low-flying plane, the sort that would stir massive amounts of anxiety in Hudson County citizens in the months after nine-one-one. Myself, I've never been voided of that anxiety. Each of those planes, I imagine in catastrophic detail, is coming for my rooftop with the aim of making dusty human remains of me. They say in the extreme heat of wildfires bones burst.

I need some time to myself, so I go up to our bedroom under the pretense of a sleep. I cry again, smallish though—no bawling now. And I do, pillowed just so, happen to fall asleep.

The shallow dreams I have are clinical in the general sense: latticed and leafy stone urns down a long corridor. And I walk the corridor, approaching nothing.

Hubby, meanwhile, is typing in web searches. Oh! what he is gleaning: patient reviews for my urologist (no complaints beyond wait times); diameters of catheter tubes; sterilization protocol; numbing lubricants. He reads about what to expect when being catheterized. *Not painful; slight discomfort at most.* That's a direct quote he jots down on a sticky pad and sticks to the corner of his computer screen.

I wake from sleep with the urge to empty my bladder. I look like a fleshy folding chair on the toilet, keeled over. The pain—I can't.

When it ends, I lift the seat to see what the hell happened. The bowl is a swirling blood bath. Dark red and what I can only guess is tissue—black ravels of cells. It's like the look of things after a rape, I think. The feel, too.

Hubby runs up the steps—two, three at a time—and finds me on the edge of the tub, crying into and at the bloody urine.

He kneels before me, and I know his devotion. Hubby's a neat freak who hates the hair and dust of the bathroom tiles. Still, he's right there with me.

I reach to flush, because I just want this all to be gone. Hubby says *Don't*, and he fetches his digital camera. "For documentation," he says.

"This isn't right," I say, not then noticing I was mimicking the words of the nurse who wielded the catheter. My mind goes to my gran with the switch in her hand when I do notice it. She, always old, came from the Carolinas and believed discipline was something to be done unto a body.

"Why did she do this to me?" I get out.

"She clearly didn't know what she was doing," Hubby says. Not in a way to excuse her. I know what he meant, but he quickly clarifies anyway. "I mean, she's incompetent, clearly. Incompetent or criminal."

I have to pee again.

More blood. More tissue. Even more painful than the previous. Now my nerves are triggering it, too. Subsequent pissings. The red, though, runs pinkish.

Hubby calls the answering service, and the connection is so bad he needs to spell my name no less than four times. It sounds like a cipher. My cellphone number becomes a lotto drawing. Hubby's face looks like heatstroke happening.

The urologist doesn't call me back. Two more calls through the answering service, and I guess it's a case of squeaky wheeling that I finally get her on the line.

She's drowsy; I can hear the somnolence in her voice. She has no answers. *Maybe*, she says when I ask if this is normal, if it could be the result of the catheter. "Blood and tissue," I tell her. "Tissue or clotting?" she asks, and I, for the first time, let my imprecations be heard. Evasively she answers my questions, unwilling to finger the nurse.

"Bleeding through the urethra will stop on its own," she says, "unless it doesn't. In which case, you should go to the ER."

And, as we both hang up, I feel like phones should still have coiled cords—for gnawing, for strangling.

I sleep fearfully, feeling the razory cutting sensation intermittently.

I know Hubby's not sleeping. He's plotting. He tells me his plans. The next morning I know he's holding himself to it, mainly, maybe, because he thinks I call him a punk coward to my girlfriends. Which I do.

A banana is sliced into his cereal bowl, the dull butter knife doing the trick, and then he's gone.

He arrives at the urologist's office not long after they open the doors.

Hubby's prone to agonistic behavior. He's there

to make a scene: full-chested, erratic, shouting. He shouts curses, demands to speak to the doctor. He wants to see the face of the nurse. His head is swelling with thoughts. Hubby's thinking of me telling him *not so hard, only easy*, or to stop altogether. He's thinking of me telling him I'm too tired. *Not tonight*, I tell him—it seems like all the time. He's thinking of calendar pages flying to the sky, of days on days of no intimacy. He's thinking of us getting older, colder.

Or at least this is what I think he thinks. It is possible, I know, that he's just mantra-ing *protect, protect, protect*. It's possible that he's not making it about him at all. Possible that he's only trying to help my healing.

I can't be helped.

So he shouts, and he wants them to think he's nutso. The call to the cops: he wants that. He knows he'll have this all wrapped up before they get there, their cruisers aslant against the parking lines. He wants his voice to be heard, my pain to be acknowledged. He wants them to know what they've done. He uses words like *assault* and *violation*. He puts his maleness on full display, posturing in an office where only women are present.

Down the corridor and out the front entrance, there are no cops. The morning humidity combined with his adrenaline gives him a headachy swell. Androgens route through his body.

He looks to the cloudless sky and thinks of me, I think. And so he barrels his shoulder brutishly into the leafy stone urn beside the entrance. The urn crumbles and the soil and touch-me-nots and marigolds contained within spill onto the pavement. Hubby gets into our family car and drives off.

There's a railroad crossing between the urologist's office and our home. Hubby has to pause for the flashing lights as the boom barrier comes down. He watches the train pass, nothing romantic. It's not a freight train. No hoboing there. Just a NJ Transit passenger train, window after window refracting the faces of working class zeroes. And he hopes, I hope, for a transcendence that won't destroy him.

Evergreen

THE OLD MAN WAS JACKED, formidable. He showed it with his cut-off t-shirt, the shoulders of which flared out and created a superhero design. He was bald, too—the bowling ball variety, turtle waxed. Liver spot here, liver spot there.

He stood with his fists on his hips and stared at the steps from the sidewalk. He didn't see Georgia sitting on the porch—maybe it was his glaucomaed vision, maybe it was the dust and pollen collected in the screens. She'd hose them down before the season ended.

She thought nothing of his staring at first, nothing much. Georgia just assumed the old man was early onset. That, or he was taking a breather on his walk. But he was so tan and muscly she figured he would've been in shape enough not to need a break. She played these process of elimination games in her head, letting her Belva Plain rest in her lap.

Georgia lifted the can of soda from the table, gulped, and watched the old man to see if it got a reaction.

Nothing.

The old man was still standing there, statue-still. His shorts were cut-off too, she noticed. How odd. What kind of a madman takes scissors to his wardrobe like that? Tangled threads and frayed fabric like so many sea anemone tentacles.

It was late summer and so hot the asphalt had that sour smell to it. Georgia wanted nothing more than to drive down the shore, but Jack was full of excuses—sea lice, west wind flies, shit bacteria (he called it *entero-coccus*, though, because he's a fucking know-it-all). So she was here, on the porch, sipping a fine, luke-cold, caffeinated beverage, increasingly concerned about the mystery man on her stoop.

The real reason Jack didn't want to go down the shore was because he felt they had to "tighten up," is how he put it. He meant the deck in back, the boards—they needed to be powerwashed, sanded, and stained. He meant the backsplash in the kitchen. She agreed on that—she hated the look of the exposed laths, made her feel roachy. He meant the busted gutter not far from where Georgia was sitting at present. She could see the dangling aluminum from her rocker.

A storm had sent a mother-of-all-branches onto their roof, crushing the gutter like a guardrail gets from a car wreck. Jack insisted on working extra shifts at AGL. He wanted the gutter repaired fast. Georgia thought the more hours he put in at AGL, the more likely he was to blow-up. So many gases in so many cylinders on that lot, and negligent forklift operators. She always believed there was nothing worse, nothing more disgraceful, than a closed casket wake. She'd never forgive the world if Jack went up in a gas explosion. Jack didn't want to be a homeowner with a gutter hanging off his roof for years, he said. Georgia could only fight him so much.

The old man wasn't looking at the gutter, though. He was staring into space, staring at her house. Like he was hoping to open the porch door with his mind.

Georgia caught a whiff of fetid air from the neighbor's steps—the butts scrunched in the coffee can that got rained on the night before.

She rotated her wrist to check the time, tapped her toes, and stood up.

"Can I help you with something?"

The look on the old man's face proved to her he

hadn't seen her until just then. He pointed at her, lazily, his arm and finger not as stiff and strong as she thought they'd be.

"I made those," he said.

"What's that?" Georgia asked, turning her head like she was hard of hearing.

"Built those," he said. "I built those."

Georgia's face must've told him how confused she was.

"The steps," he said, "I built those steps."

Okay, she thought. Definitely senile.

The old man tilted his head back and forth, and his lip inched up his cheek.

"Maybe ten, eleven years ago."

"We bought the house about seven ago," she told him, "in November," as if it mattered.

"They look good," he said. "They look good, no?"

"Yes," Georgia said. "They're fine. No problems."

She recognized she was clipping her speech to match the way he talked.

"I'm-a Giuseppe," the old man said.

Georgia touched her fingers to where her neck pitched into her chest. "Georgia," she said.

She noticed the old man's sneakers were sideways. They hadn't kept their shape, and his feet snuggled into them awkwardly. They looked like they'd been worn to slippers. It was the only part of his outfit that seemed less than taut. He cinched his lips with his fingers, thinking. The nails looked dirty, or at least browned with age.

"People no take care of their property," he said. "They buy the house, don't care for it, and move. Just like that," he said, "they move." His hand showed how.

"Yes, that's true," she said, though she didn't feel strongly about it one way or the other.

"I live down the block," he said, "near to the library."

The way he said *library* made her laugh through her nose. He made the word sound like it had seven *r*'s and they all drawled together. Georgia realized she was standing sentinelly in the doorway with her arms crossed. By now she was trusting her gut again, and it told her, breathily, the old man could be trusted. So she undid her arms and leaned against the doorframe, but she felt that didn't go far enough, and she sublimated to a sitting position on the top step.

"I go to the library a lot," she told him, as if this was of consequence. "I just picked one up from there, *Evergreen*."

"People no take care of their property," he said again. "Just splish splosh trash everywhere," he waved. A look of genuine and unbearable disgust attacked his face, seized him.

"I've probably passed your house," Georgia said.

"These people," he said, "they move from the next town over…" He searched and struggled to summon the name, even snapping his fingers to bring it into existence, but couldn't recall it. Georgia knew the town but didn't give it to him.

"They, these people, they don't have a respect of a property."

A woman was walking by with her dog. Georgia knew her insofar as she knew the woman was always fixated on her phone screen. That, and she held the dog leash looped in her hand. Georgia hated that, but at least she picked up the shit where it fell.

The dog—it was a beastly cur she allowed to run free—accosted the old man's legs, nosing his shins and calves, sniffing his swollen sneakers. Georgia thought the dog might run his pockets.

"Down boy," the woman said. "Down now. C'mon now."

The old man patted the dog's haunches. There was the brawn Georgia had sensed. His pats clapped and sent tufts of fur floating into the air like dandelion puffs.

"He's a good boy," the old man said. "Yessa, he's a good boy."

The dog finally obeyed the woman's command.

"That's alright," the old man said. "That is a alright."

He moved closer up the walkway toward Georgia.

She stood up again. The old man had on enough cologne to chloroform a cow.

"My wife," he said, "she passed. Bless, bless."

"I'm sorry to hear that," Georgia said, uncrossing her arms. She touched the top of her head like she remembered she'd forgotten something.

"Bless," the old man said. "She always say to me, she say: 'Giusepp, you work too hard. You need to come home sooner. Love, love. Come home to me my love,' she say."

Georgia said, "That's sweet." She laced her fingers together and held her hands at her waist, cradling the old man's eulogy.

"Cancer," he pointed at his body, nowhere specific. "She had it for, oh, six, seven months."

"That's terrible," Georgia said. She thought of how awful her responses were. How inadequate they must sound to him.

"Bless, though," he said. "The hospital, our home. The doctors, they let her come home. I was sitting right there next to her," he pointed at the sidewalk, "when she passed. Bless."

"I'm so happy to hear that," she said. "The hospitals don't always do that. They'll keep you there. I'm happy you got to share that moment with your wife."

"Share that moment," the old man said. "Bless."

Georgia became hot and she felt a stinging under her arms. The clouds moved, and what was so far an overcast day suddenly became blazing. The old man's skin looked even worse in the sunlight, and Georgia found herself wishing he'd move and find some shade.

"The steps," he said, "they good?"

"Yes," Georgia said. "They're crumbling a bit under the bottom one there, on the side. But it's nothing to worry about."

The old man approached now, and it was only the steps between them. He hunched over, hands on knees, and examined the area.

"I think it's fine," Georgia said. "It's not a big problem. Wear and tear."

"It's no good," he said, wagging his finger. He bent down again, touched his lips, and then the crumbled mortar. "Needs to be patched up here. I get my bucket."

"No, I think it's fine," she said, worried he would actually do something.

"I do the repair," he said.

"It's fine," she said. "I think it'll be okay. I've got to ask Jack about it before anything."

"Who's Jack?" the old man asked. "You husband?"

"Yes," she said. "He'll be home soon, hopefully."

"It's no charge," the old man said. "You husband will be surprised. He'll like the work. He knows the repair."

"I don't know," Georgia said. She moved backwards, off the steps and onto the porch again.

"I get my bucket," he said. She guessed this meant for cement, for mortar? She didn't know. "You husband be happy. I do a good job."

"Could you come back later?" she asked him. Georgia really wanted to return to her book. She hadn't even stopped at the end of a paragraph, which always annoyed her.

"It'll be a nice surprise for you husband," he said. "For Jackie. My wife," he went on, "she loved it—*loved* it—when I do a job for her, fix this, fix that, without her at the house. She came back and said, *Thank you, thank you, thank you, Giusepp. You make our home so beautiful.* Bless."

Georgia found the way he spoke about his wife so adorable, so full of ardor, she almost couldn't take it. It made her a bit queasy. In the pit of her stomach she felt something—an aching, a trembling. The sun's heat was folding over her like a sheet blowing through porch windows.

She couldn't stop him. She didn't know how. His wife was dead. Bless. Jack would understand.

The Ice Caverns

CYNTHIA, LET ME TELL you this. Sex with Philly remains the best—the *bestest*, my bestie. I don't tell you this to brag (I know you're as sex-starved as my mom—not as hopeless, though!); I tell you this because it's become a real problem. Like, how'm I supposed to break it off with this fucker if he can still make me see celestial and sparkly stars in the sack? Sure, this is the same douchebag who had me standing in my parents' tub, the water only a few inches high, lapping against my ankles. The same sorority chick stalker that had me holding the hair dryer at my shoulder, negative ions swirling around my fuzzy brain. The cheater who had me waiting to hear the splash into the basin and the death sizzle afterwards. But he's so cute, Cynth! He's so electro*cute*. (I'm kidding, for fuck's sake—*relax*.) And this killer cuteness and boot-knocking deftness somehow supersedes his opioid dependency. What can I say, slut? He's my junkie in shining armor. Chinks up and down.

I know, *I know!* I'm flippant right now because I'm post-fuck. That wispy cotton candy lightheadedness. True. Nonetheless, as the ether wears off, I can describe to you the non-paradisiacal shit, too. Of which there is much. And we can't just blame it on holiday depression. I'm willing to be as cheery as 106.7 Lite FM induces me to be. (Christmas songs are shit, Cynth.)

Philly was driving my car—I let him. Thought it would be funny to watch him swerve in and out of traffic the way he does with those plush reindeer antlers attached to the windows on the Mazda. Tiffy was sitting shotgun while I sat in back holding the baby to my Forever 21 puffer jacket for body warmth. Jamie was sitting in his car seat next to me, too big for it to be buckled.

The car filled with chilly, freezing, brick-ass air because Philly rolled the driver's side window down. He didn't like how some Sussex County hick in a GMC pickup was riding him, so he shouted some choice words into the wind as the truck passed. Either his words cut through the velocity or his crazed facial expression did the conveying, because the redneck slowed to our speed and middle-fingered Philly right back.

Not one to be outdone, Philly started searching the cupholder for toll change. And you know where Route 46 splits with 80 and 23, right Cynthia? Philly's steering with his knees and zipping quarters, nickels, and pennies out the window at this Duck Dynasty motherfucker. You could hear the coins ricocheting off the pickup. Tiffy's got her knees pulled to her chin in complete fear. I'm smacking Philly from the backseat as baby Elise starts bawling in my lap. Jamie is hopping up and down, cheering his deadbeat daddy on like a typical boys-will-be-boys boy.

This is our family portrait, Cynth. Merry, merry with Philly road-raging and those plush reindeer antlers in the way of his coin tossing.

Somehow we arrived unmangled by windshield shards and twisted metal at Jody's Florist and Patio. You know the Ice Caverns, right? You grew up the same kind of poor I did, so you know the cheap thrill of chintzy Christmas decorations and buzzing animatronic display cases. My kids are gonna experience it the same as we did. You know I'm a nostalgia whore.

Philly strutted across the parking lot leaving me dragging along the three no-necked monsters. He was feeling like a million bucks because he just got a windfall (a few thousand, if you're curious—and I know you are) from a lithium-ion battery exploding in his pants pocket. The thing was in his e-cig and rubbed just right and shot off like a fireworks display from his crotch. Just like those stories you see on Channel 7 News. His thigh blackened like batwings with second-degree burns, and he's got to have one of his dopehead buddies at the halfway house lather the wound with ointment three times a day. So it's glossed and gauzed and he tells everyone he's an invalid.

Whenever I'm mad at him, like I was right then, I see him in the negativest light. He's skeleton thin with sunken cheeks and blotchy skin. He's ghost-pale. He stinks like cabbage and gasoline. He's unimpressive in all aspects. That new lamb leather bomber jacket from Macy's be damned.

I caught up and passed baby Elise off to him. She koala-clutched him because she's too little to know who's deserving of her affection and who's not. Kids are impartial like that. I know you know. Your little ones probably love their Montessori teachers more than their mama, right? How the hell do you afford that shit, anyway? You ho.

We passed right by the coin-operated rides outside the store. No way I was trekking back to our Africa-far parking spot for quarters (or what was left of them from

Philly's highway donations). Jamie was whining for the helicopter ride—I swear if that kid isn't ADHD already.

The line for Santa's lap wound through velvet ropes and beyond. Tiffy was tugging on my jacket pocket, and Jamie was knocking breakable ornaments off a silver-white tree. I wasn't about to pay for broken merchandise. Wasn't about to wait two hours for Kris Bonerpants Kringle either. Fuck that. So we paid the admission fee to the Ice Caverns and entered the insurance-claim-waiting-to-happen maze of sheetrock and particleboard.

As soon as you walk in, they've got you facing a fake brick wall of commemorative bricks. They've "etched" (inkjet printed) names of financial donors onto these "bricks" (pieces of paper). *Thank you to all our loyal family of supporters over the years!!!* it says. With the three exclamation points and all. I wonder what it must be like to be them: money donors. I wonder what it must be like to be one who donates in the name and honor of a pet. "For Sprinkles: the best XMAS GIFT we ever got! MEOWY CHRISTMAS!" Philly and me chuckled to each other.

Philly was holding Elise so close to his face that I was afraid his oxy o'clock shadow would give her pristine, chubby cheeks a reaction. She's got sensitive skin, like him. Me with the good genes, I can lay out in the sun and turn tanning-bed bronze in minutes.

He held her up high in hopes she could see the display behind the plexiglass. It was a Disney arrangement. They've got stuffed animals thrown in there amongst the fluffy cotton snow. Crudely painted wooden cutouts of characters, too. And Philly *oohed* and *ahhed* for Elise, saying, "Look, El, Daffy Duck." And I corrected him, "Donald"—you idiot.

I know. Petty, right? That's what you're thinking, Cynth. But you get where I'm coming from. He's uninformed. And he's uninformed because he's absent as hell, out of the picture. If he was around even remotely enough he'd know the difference between a Daffy and a Donald.

So that soured me for the duration of the Ice Caverns experience. Granted it only takes about seven minutes to walk through—ten if there's traffic, which there was. This Brady Bunch in front of us insisted on cherishing each moment and taking a million fucking pictures on three different iPhones. They blocked the way. We couldn't pass them. They'd huddle together after each display case to marvel at their shared genetic triumph captured in each photo. Like, earth to Marcia Brady! Trying to move along here. I hate people, Cynth. You know I hate people.

The tour of the Ice Caverns slogged on. We passed the Styrofoam snowmen, the peppermint-patterned wrapping paper wallpaper, the evergreen tablecloth spread, the waving Mrs. Claus, and the slumbering Santa Claus. "That's mummy Santa," Philly told Tiffy and Jamie. I shushed him, because the last thing I need to deal with is Jamie having nightmares again like he did around Halloween. And then we got held up at the skating pond display because our pro-athlete-to-be Jamie can't pitch a penny into a wide-open space to save his life. He was in tears when he finally got one to splash in.

By the time we arrived at the religious-as-fuck displays, I was exhausted. I'd had my fill of glitter and ribbons and cellophane and garland. All the decorations are so old—ancient even. The baby Jesus in his manger and his definitely-not-a-whore virgin mom and cuckold dad had faces cracking at the cheekbones. Neither me or Philly are as Catholic as we were raised, so the kids asked a gazillion questions about these decidedly non-festive animatronic characters.

"It's just something some people believe," I told Tiffy. She wanted to know why, of course. "Just because," I said. "Because they're dumb. Because they like stories."

And, of course, I had forgotten the 9/11 memorial display that comes after the religious shit. More questions. *Why are there skyscrapers, Mom? Why is there a firetruck?* I hustle them through, ignoring the questions. Then Philly just piles on, because apparently I'm the complaints department.

"My thigh is killing me," he said.

"What's the matter?"

"These jeans are chafing at my burn. Can you carry El?"

He passed the little one over to me, and from that point until we got back into the car he was worthless. I'm corralling the two older ones away from the coin-operated rides again with Elise hanging off my hip. And Philly was up ahead, really selling the limp now, not looking back (which, I got to say, is just *so* perfectly symbolic of his role in our family). He's a real Orpheus, alright. I could fall headfirst into a nest of vipers and he'd be none the wiser.

•

I have zero interest, Cynth—*zero*—in upholding traditions. I was subjected to endless traditions growing up, and they were just miserable. Traditions are obligations, I say. My mom was always too full of Catholic guilt to abandon them, so she instead decided to carry out traditions on misery mode. Still, it's somehow becoming a tradition for us to go to Bruno's for dinner and then drive around Upper Montclair looking at Christmas lights.

Bruno's, because Philly insists their Sicilian slices are unparalleled. I couldn't care less. You know me, Cynth: I get chicken fingies and fries just the same as the kids.

We feasted, and Elise took an applesauce squeeze pouch to the face. Everyone was contented.

The waitress gave Tiffy and Jamie coloring book pages and crayons. Tiffy had a near-meltdown because her page had a tear, and Jamie was flipping shit because he didn't get the crayon colors he wanted. I told him to color the reindeer green and get over it.

I needed a deep breath and a spa visit. Crayon scarcity is a real problem in restaurants, Cynthia! It's not funny—*stop laughing!* And for Christ's sake, so many diners are resorting to those three-colors-in-one triangle-shaped crayons nowadays. You know the ones I'm talking about. Those bitches snap under the least bit of applied pressure. Like give my kids something of quality to distract them or give them nothing at all. Donate to my iPad fund so I can keep them in a screen-coma until the teen years. *Please!*

Midway through dinner and Philly dropped his Sicilian slice to his plate—clattering utensils and everything. He lifts Elise from his lap and plops her on mine. This, all because he spied two NA friends slumped at the counter near the front—Dopioid Crisis Walking and Dead Man Doping for all I know or care.

Unattractive is how he looked with his arms around his bosom buddies, his fellow H-trainhoppers, his horseback riders. I don't know what they were talking about, but each of them had the junky slouch going on. Philly pinched French fries from one of their plates. Took a swig of Coke from the other. Elise dropped her paci to the floor, and I was stretching to reach it. I eventually had to stand up to retrieve it, which got a glance from Philly. I made my displeasure known by giving the stinkiest stink-eye I've ever summoned. I dunked Elise's paci into Philly's glass of water to let him know he was fucking up. He seemed to get the message, because he said his so-longs and hustled back to our table and started shoving food into his meth mouth.

There wasn't much talking between me and him for the rest of the meal, only the exchange of awkward facial expressions when the check arrived. (I paid—shocker.) We piled back into the Mazda, same seating arrangement as before, and hopped on 46 for a few minutes until the exit for Upper Montclair. Jamie kept rolling down the window, so I had to smack the back of his head. It didn't hurt none—he was wearing a beanie. But my reach jarred the baby, and she started crying from that and the frigid cold her dumbass brother let in.

Philly idled the car down the side streets. These are streets with cobblestoned curbs, so you should know what's up. You wouldn't know it because you always believe the best about people, Cynth—always believe people are capable of amazing feats—but the owners of these lavish homes (let's call them "Richard" and "Karen") didn't even string up their own displays. The landscapers do it all— ladders to the rooftops, holly on the railings, extension cords running the length of the lush lawn to keep inflatable penguins and sleighs inflated. They've got nativity scenes with real straw, real wood construction (fake baby Jesus, though). It's elaborate, and it's a sight, and every mansion nowadays seems to have those projector lights that make lasers dance across the siding.

The kids gawked at the lights—they love that shit. I like it, too. I like to see the colors reflected in the windshield. You've got to catch it at the right angle. It hasn't snowed yet this winter, so the decorations on the houses attract all the attention. No winter wonderland to compete with. I don't want it to snow this winter, Cynth. I rather everything be cold and dead without the sludge. I can't see how anybody'd want the snow. All it does is pile up on the roadsides after the plows come through, and then it blackens from the exhaust fumes and the oil leaks. The sky can keep its snow. I don't want it.

·

The kids were spent when we pulled up to our apartment. I say "our" as if Philly has a presence there, as though he's contributing to the rent check. Elise is asleep in my arms and Tiffy and Jamie are dragging their feet to the building entrance. Jaime doesn't even tap each name on the clusterbox like he usually does. Philly scoops him up and bends him over his shoulder like a duffel bag. I stare up at the brickface of the building and see our third-floor apartment window. It's the living room window, and I've got it decorated with icicle lights. One of the suction cups had come loose though, and the string of lights drooped down. Depressing.

We put the kids to bed without any baths. Tiffy was happy about that; Jaime complained (he wanted to play with his Paw Patrol toys) but only until his head hit the pillow. Elise woke up when I stripped her and put the sleep-sack on, but I rubbed her head from crown to brow and it soothed her back to rest.

I was still pissed about the abandonment at the pizzeria, so I just wanted Philly to bounce back to the halfway house. But he came at me with, *Aww, I don't want to wait for the bus* and *Aww, it's such a long ways to Keansburg.* Which really means: *Aww, can't we smash?*

And we did. (Don't be judgy, Cynth—judgment-free zone, please!)

I've got myself looking good, girl. I P90X-it-up after the kids go to sleep. Then I take a bowl of cookies-and-cream to the face, but still. I'm not trying to be one of those skinny bitches with the thigh gap. Shit's gross, Cynthia. They look like the skeleton that used to stand in Overby's science lab.

Can I tell you something? Philly is hardened, right? When he used to work heavy construction (when he used to work, period), he was always chapped, sun-dried. But his mouth softens during sex. The hardness of his chin and cheeks recedes back and leaves a baby-mouth of gentleness like all the plush that populates the kids' room. It's so sweet, Cynthia. I can't stand it. I freakin' swoon.

We had a real go of it. A true bacchanal. The sort of sex that starts in the bed and ends on the floor. But our floor is hardwood, so we ended in the bed. It was dark, the sky clear, so the moonlight actually lit up the room like in a rom-com love scene. We've always excelled at sex, which—if I'm being honest-to-Godest—that's helped us get past a lot in our relationship. You know this already, though. So do our neighbors, ceiling and floor. We just vibrate when we couple up, entangled—two backs beasting.

It was like an out-of-body experience next to the orange warmth of the space heater. I sometimes fanta-size of electrical fire sparking and us going up in flames mid-coitus like two candles too close and the flames flick-ering through each other. That would smooth our rough edges, purify our match. Or it could just end the drama. Because—said it before, will say it again—I feel like I could rip him to shreds sometimes. And my climactic, orgasmic, asthmatic ecstasy blunts, dulls, and thuds when the moonlight catches Philly's thigh just right and I see his lithium-ion burn shimmer like sheet metal. And with that image of his thigh-burn I see a million child support checks shoveled with one of those old-school metal snow shovels into an incinerator. Fuck, Philly.

He fell asleep before I did (a shocking statement in the history of heterosexual eroticism, if there ever was one). But I fell asleep shortly after. It wasn't hard. I was parent-tired and exhausted with the holiday rushing, the psychodrama, and the muscle exertion. When I woke up a few hours later to pee, Cynthia, he was gone. So was the Mazda. He stole it. Under the cover of night—like a ski-masked thief. I called the cops on him, Cynthia. I've got to tell you, girl: I don't even care.

Sleep Mode

Whenever Nasreen dreamed of work, she dreamed of it from the outside. There was the office building in Paramus, and all of its five floors were gutted and charred and windowless—nothing but a skeletal frame remaining. Moss and rot climbing its exterior walls, foresting it. There weren't any cars congested on the highway behind where she stood—not a carbon coughing one, but she could see the clouds on the opposite side of the building by looking clear through the blasted out windows. She got no closer than that. Her feet were a plinth in the dream, and she herself was a greened sculpture, immobile and possessing a stiffness she could feel in her sleep like a leg cramp.

The dream was different of late, though. She sat in traffic, her smartphone tucked into the fold of her hijab, taking calls before she even arrived at the office. She was always the first employee to arrive, and it was that same way in the dream. She set to work immediately, loading the software on her desktop and massaging her wrist, rigorously pressing her carpal bones in an established pattern. The wait cursor spun on the welcome page of the program, and she had the same thought she always had while watching it: a longing for the outdated hourglass that used to turn itself over, stippled with pixelated sand.

One eye didn't work so well—it sort of slid south-east—so she had to lean in close to the monitor screen, squinting. She always looked as if she were whispering secrets to it. *Sweet nothings*, Jonathan from payroll said once. He'd caught her lips moving only inches from the screen. She was mortified, withdrew, and slumped into the mesh of her ergonomic chair. Jonathan must've seen how red her cheeks got, bleeding through her foundation, but he was relentless, adding, *You're liable to fog the glass, Reeny.*

The algorithms scrolled up and down Nasreen's monitor. She fixated on the arrows, the right angles at which they turned and redirected. Her good eye momentarily blurred, but she rubbed the blear away with her fist, and she continued scanning: variables, square brackets, and the basest geometric shapes. Nasreen obsessed over all of it—doing her job, doing her job *well*.

When coworkers began to arrive—some sharply on-time, others slightly late—Nasreen kept on with her clicking and coding but still managed to smile at each of them. She was cordial, of course, but she could be cordial without falling off-task. She would be held to account for her time—management kept tabs: they had remote access to her screen, to her web history, and the infrared security camera high up on the wall across the room, there was that.

Nasreen's work was interrupted by her manager, his disembodied voice arriving over the intercom. *Nasreen,* the voice said, ghostlike, *bring me the file.* The statement repeated over and over again, eventually disintegrating into only the word *bring.* The word stretched, its consonants dragging metallically over the intercom. *Brrrring.* This, until Nasreen woke and recognized the rotary phone ringtone on her smartphone. She lifted onto her elbow, answered the call, and swept the hair out of her face—it was staticky, the strands stretching to the pillow like filaments in a plasma lamp. A rep from the Pacific Time Zone putting in overtime—midnight in the west; three in the east. Nasreen woke with her brain already running on job logic, so she had his questions fielded in seconds. There was no going back to sleep, though. She was up now, nervy and wired.

That was the fourth night in a row with that dream. Nasreen wasn't just standing outside the ruins of her workplace—she was inside it, working. It was as real as feeling the frayed patch of gray carpeting beneath her desk where her heels pivot and her toes grind. As real as that quiet explosion of synthetic fibers in the ashlar pattern, hidden from sight like the power strip. It was her habit to wear athletic socks because her feet would sweat in dress ones. Management never saw that either. There were things, she reasoned, one should keep private.

She couldn't fall back to sleep once she'd been jarred by a call or a text. And she never took steps to prevent the interruptions. If anything, she enabled them. Her routine was to check email before bed—whether an alert sounded or not—organizing her inbox according to *Read*, *Unread*, and *Flagged*. Deleted items were never deleted, only moved to designated folders. Her account, she estimated, had to be scratching at its last gigs of free storage.

She'd exfoliate her face, and it was that brief moment she counted as rest and relaxation, as leisure, as yoga, as gym, as shrink, as beach read, and as spa. The submersion of her face in the shallow basin of her palms—that rinsing, she convinced herself, was all the renewal she needed.

Next, she'd arrange her devices at her bedside—her smartphone, laptop, alarm clock, and lamp all plugged into the same strip. If she was awakened by a call—which translated into a task—she was at the ready. The laptop never shut down; always in sleep mode. Her *Sent* folder was full of emails time-stamped with ungodly hours.

Once awakened, Nasreen liked to sit at the kitchen table with a cup of tea. She steeped sage leaves in it as her mother always did. It was how all her brothers' and sisters' tummy aches were treated when they were little.

Her own children—Mansour, who she called Man, and Emmy—were sleeping serenely in their bedrooms. She had white noise machines outside the doors of both their rooms—they'd been there since the kids were infants. The collage of frequencies was as comforting to them, she felt, as their security blankets and stuffed animals. Nasreen liked the sound, too. She liked how the home hummed.

She clicked on the TV and watched an infomercial on mute. The web address at the bottom of the screen was for CulinaryCuts.net, but they weren't selling kitchen knives. There were no cooking demonstrations going on. The camera didn't capture the host's face, just his rough hands turning over lethal weaponry. Close-ups of rolled sleeves and knobbed fingers fanning out blades, files, and openers from pocketknives. The host showcased a set that included bowie knives, spear-points, butternut bone knives, and a Viking sword. For Nasreen, who'd been brought to the states when she was only weeks old, it was a world of violence so foreign it was almost fiction.

The closed captions overlapped the toll free number—Nasreen squinted (her weak eye having all but slid into her skull) to read what was being said. *If you dial now…*, the host exhorted. *An incredible blade… Our lowest price ever…Biggest liquidation ever offered.* The merchandise was displayed on motorized racks. Exclusive items rotated on plexiglass platforms.

She lowered the TV volume to only a few fluorescent green bars—she'd been through this often enough to know what was loud—and then unmuted. She heard a cacophony of ringing telephones foregrounded by the host's honeysuckle sweet Southern accent. *Beautiful mirror polishing!* he said, caressing a dagger blade. A countdown clock in the lower right corner of the screen let Nasreen know she was running out of time on this once in a lifetime deal.

Mansour ordered a samurai sword off eBay once. Fadi ripped into his son and took the Xbox controllers away for a month. Nasreen pleaded with her husband to go easier on Man, who was only nine at the time. Fadi grunted as he shoved the controllers into the darkest reaches of his sock drawer. *You were the one who left the credit card info in there*, Nasreen had told her husband.

She turned off the TV and heard the silent hum of the home again. Her body sunk into the corner of the sectional. She swept the nap of the suede cushions back and forth, shading and brightening it with the path of her fingertips. She swished the dregs in her teacup, only the slightest liquid running over the sage leaves. Fadi hated when she placed her cup in the sink with the leaves still in it. He was the one, he complained, that always had to pinch them out and carry them dripping to the trash bin. Somehow it was her fault they didn't spring for the garbage disposal when they had the kitchen redone. For all his grumbling, though, Nasreen missed Fadi terribly. She'd take his bellyaching about sage leaves over being companionless on the couch any day. Even though she rarely allowed herself to be comforted, she appreciated how he combed over her hair, pausing to gently squeeze the tension from her head. *You need to take it easy*, he'd tell her.

But now Fadi was with family in Jordan, having been deported even after they sunk three thousand dollars into an immigration lawyer. He had resisted filing paperwork with the registry and was theatrically and forcibly removed from their property. Officers dragged him down the walkway for a distance, his rigid legs brushing against the azaleas and leaving a trail of petals along the pavers. Nasreen got down onto her knees the next morning, gathered the red petals into her palms, and funneled them into an envelope. She missed Fadi's hand on the back of her head. Missed his solicitous words. His emails were cold. She took them less seriously, less to heart, than his spoken support. She kept the open envelope of azalea petals on the kitchen countertop, pinched between the sugar and flour canisters.

•

Sunday night—what Nasreen called Monday Eve—Fadi appeared in her dream. He was in a black suit, dour as a pallbearer, and driving her to work. She was in the passenger seat and there was a sea of knives at her feet—she couldn't even see the floor mat. Fadi wasn't saying much, focused instead on the endless circles he was making around her ruinous office building, which, again, appeared with its windowless, war zone architecture. Nasreen was desperate to keep her feet elevated off the floor, off the sharp and glinting knives. *Would you just relax already?* Fadi finally said to her. And so she let her feet fall, a pair of stiletto heels (which she had never owned and would never wear) piercing the medley of blades.

Then she was at her desk. There she was, a full four hours before she'd be alarmed to wakefulness—coerced into showering, making-up, and commuting by misty market forces—and she was already working in her dreams. Her unconscious mind began sorting through cryptic and unsolvable sequences on a screen she wasn't even staring at—a cognitive apparition. A mental glitch. She woke up suffering what a web search would soon determine was a panic attack: palpitations, sticky sweat, dizziness, and—what sounded and felt scariest of all—*derealization*.

Nasreen was upright with blurry vision and confused. She flipped over her pillow and started sweeping away what she believed was a commotion of bugs—ants, millipedes, silver fish, and cockroaches. Her arm swept them off the sheet and onto the floor. She came to, speaking bombastic, tongue-tied nonsense. Some markup language fallen into disuse.

Once she had calmed down—a face wash, a cup of sage tea, an email to Fadi describing what had happened—she went about her morning routine as usual, which was a comfort to her.

She couldn't help but fall off-task at work though, and she beat herself up, all but self-flagellated. Her mouse may as well have been a flail.

Logging out of her personal email, she was sidetracked by article headlines—just trash, celebrity news. She scrolled in a way that protected her from the watchful eyes of passersby and surveillance. If she could only manage to keep the browser full of text, words followed by words, it could easily be mistaken for metadata, not the latest divorce filings and botched plastic surgeries of the rich and famous. If she kept away from flashy head-lines and paparazzi photos—even the most innocuous of which, by her standards, would be NSFW—she could get away with a few moments of psychic relief.

But she couldn't escape the banner ads running vertically down the side of her screen. There it was: a silver-haired woman working a hula-hoop around her hips, gleefully advertising adult diapers. Nasreen had made an innocent internet purchase months ago for her poor, incontinent mother. *Months ago!* She'd done nothing so cruel as to be so bedeviled for so long after. She x'd out of the browser window and got back to mazelike algorithms.

She had a post-it note on her desk under her key-board, a quote of compliment from upper-management. It was chicken-scratched so only she could read it. She was proud, sure, but modest. Mr. Stinson's words were for her and her alone. And she read them whenever she needed an extra boost to work through a coffee break in order to meet a deadline. She read it now, feeling the back of it, how its adhesive strip had all but lost its stickiness to fuzz and her fingerprints. She slid it back under the keyboard, stiffened her spine, squinted at the monitor screen, and accidentally clonked her head against the glass.

An email alert seemed to synchronize with the sound of skull meeting monitor. Nasreen opened her inbox and discovered a short message from her husband.

RE: panic attack?
They don't pay you enough, Nasreen. Not for all this.
Fadi

Mr. Stinson arrived out of nowhere. "You don't look well, Nasreen," he said. "Why don't you take the afternoon?" She'd been caught, of course. What was she thinking? Her screen was being watched on some other screen behind some two-way mirror. Her shifty movements had been noticed, flagged—it was probably that unblinking lens on the infrared security camera. Her one eye slid southeast. She felt ashamed.

As she shuffled and packed her things, she couldn't face Mr. Stinson. She'd been unproductive. She clicked off her monitor, and the darkened screen showed an oily smudge where her forehead had made contact.

•

She didn't know what to do with herself. Home, she deeply felt, wasn't an option. There was still a trace of disquiet from the morning's panic attack scene, and the place—with the kids at school and the light coming through the windows at an angle she didn't typically witness—was ghostly. Home was for the practice of rituals, but what ritual was to be performed at eleven in the morning?

So she drove the opposite direction she normally drove, heading west instead of east. She remembered reading nineteenth century novels in college, how there were always quack doctors telling hysterical women to recuperate in the fresh air of the country. It wasn't spring—there were still plenty of nasty roadside snow heaps speckled with gravel—but the sun was shining, and it gave the impression of warmth. Nasreen turned off the highway, followed signs uphill, and slowed her speed when she entered the Garret Mountain Nature Reservation.

Joggers jogged and walkers walked, but regardless of speed, they all bundled their faces with scarves and furry collars. One man had his hood pulled so tightly all that remained of his face was a set of eyes peering through a small oval. Nasreen glanced at the clock on her dash. *Don't these people work?* she thought.

There was an equestrian center just off the road, and Nasreen leaned over her passenger seat to see the horses feeding off hay bales stacked against the split-rail fence. Most had heavy, plaid blankets draped over their backs, and it made Nasreen think of the cover of the JCPenney catalog at Christmas time. A car honked at Nasreen so she pulled into the pedestrian lane. She watched the horses for a little while longer and then continued along the one-way road.

She parked in the overlook lot—a semi-circle of spaces, each providing a vast view of Paterson below. The man in the vehicle next to her smoked a cigarette and ashed out of a sliver of open window. The young couple in the Civic on her other side were reclined so that she couldn't see their faces or torsos, only their arms and fingers working rapidly on their phones.

The view was remarkable, but it was a shame it looked out onto Paterson, Nasreen thought. There was so little natural beauty, so little green, just brown and gray industrial squalor—smokestacks and the interstate. She was glad she didn't live there. She felt lucky to live where she did. She had relatives in Paterson, and Fadi used to buy halal meat at a shop on Market Street, but once the kids were of school age, they rarely found a good enough reason to visit.

Nasreen observed the activity of the parking lot. Carloads of people arrived and hurried from the warmth of their vehicles to a pair of coin-operated binoculars. Someone would dash back to the car to scrounge the floor mats, console, and glove compartment for loose change. The others would wait, working the swivel on the viewer, trying to locate their homes far below. Someone would drop in the quarter, and everybody would compete for a turn looking through the lenses.

Inevitably, the visitors would pose against the stone wall for photos. The wall was something very Connecticut-like, colonial and frosty, doublewide and intended to protect people from plummeting over the jagged cliff into Paterson. There was always one person, she noticed, climbing the wall, daringly walking the length of it. Usually it was a gutsy teenage boy—rangy kids who looked a lot like Mansour.

She checked her phone every time it buzzed, but she resisted answering. She kept watching a plastic bag ballooning out of a trash barrel. The bag was clamped to the lip of it, and so it whipped in the wind doing a dear life hold. One kid, with legs as long as lampposts, hopped over the wall and lighted on the littered and craggy precipice. Nasreen leaned over her steering wheel trying to follow his path. He crouched down and his friends crowded around him, bending over the sharp-edged top stones. The kid hopped back to safety, hustled to the trash barrel, and punched the plastic bag back into it. He peered inside, found nothing, but picked up an empty Dunkin' Donuts coffee cup that was on the ground beside the barrel.

The lanky kid hopped over the stone wall again, but this time he reemerged cradling an injured sparrow in the coffee cup. The bird's wing was ruffled and spasming. His friends huddled and they all gawked, some poking, at this grave and common bird sheltered in a discarded piece of garbage.

•

Nasreen crossed a meadow, lifting her knees high as she did because she feared what the tall grass might be hiding. The longer end of her hijab blew free behind her so it looked like a flag flapping on its pole. There was a charcoal black drone in the sky above her, and she glared at the middle-aged man piloting it some yards away. He seemed blissfully unconcerned with the winds of the day.

The ground evened out, flattened with fallen leaves and wisps, as she entered the forested part of the mountain. Her goal was to walk as deeply into the woods as she could without getting snagged on brambles or turning an ankle. Eventually, she was satisfied with the distance she had hiked—thankful as ever for wearing flats—and sat impishly on a boulder that seemed to perfectly contour to the curves of her body. Before her was a corridor of fallen trees, many completely yanked from the earth. Their entire root systems were exposed, and all the large and tiny entanglements were muddied with clumps of ochre clay.

The unceasing and whipping wind made her eyes water. Nasreen wiped away tears with the cuff of her jacket sleeve.

She rubbed the corner of her weak eye, and it produced an inhuman creak—something like a click, an urgent message being tapped out on a telegraph key. Morse code. Dashes and dots arising from somewhere deep inside her. *The eyes were windows, right? To the soul?* This was the tear duct she was pressing, though, where the yellow discharge had pooled the time she contracted pink eye when Emmy was only weeks old. Only a month of maternity leave, and she spent half of it with her eyes burning with bacteria. What a bust that had been.

Cars were passing on the other side of the reservation. Nasreen could see them through the leafless, bony trees. The trees were all knotty trunks and spindly limbs. Once spring arrived, she thought, that would all be lost. Those details would be blanketed with luxuriant greens.

Maybe this is what having a refuge was like, she thought. Maybe this is what people meant when they said they needed *some time* and put in for a mental health day on the calendar at the office. She felt "good," as vague as that acknowledgment was. What was more important, for her, was that she was *feeling*, period. She leaned back on the boulder, and she felt grainy particles prickle her palms. She looked to the sky through the chaos of the bare branches, all their tiny twigs tangling like the crossing-out a child does in a coloring book.

The trees swayed, some severely. Nasreen closed her watery eyes and listened to the creaking.

•

Nasreen was still hearing the creaking of the trees when she woke in a hospital bed, swimming in a hospital gown, with her younger sister, Jana, standing over her. At first, she thought it was Fadi. But Jana's knife-sharp cheekbones soon cut through the blurriness of her vision.

She was barely conscious, and her voice—she soon discovered—was a whisper. It hurt to even move her mouth. The tip of her tongue was so dry she thought it might split. Her legs were stiff, she realized, braced and elevated under the bed sheets. Her arms were free to move, but they were bruised up to the elbows, bursts of purple spreading under her fair skin. She struggled to lift her head, and when she did, Jana was quick to tell her *Don't*.

"You had an accident," her sister said.

She repeated the word *accident* back to Jana, but all she managed to pronounce was the final syllable.

Her hand—punctured with an IV, the tubes running up her arm situated with transparent medical tape—reached toward her head. Her fingertips felt the thick and layered gauze wrapped around her throbbing skull.

"What were you doing in the woods?" Jana asked. "You were lucky anybody even found you there."

"Woods?" Nasreen said. She imagined the drone-pilot running to her aid, the controller dropping from his hand into the tall grass of the meadow.

A doctor entered the room, her stethoscope dangling from her neck.

"A tree came down on you, Nasreen. From the winds," Jana said. "But you're awake now. You're awake now." She moved aside for the doctor.

Nasreen didn't hear what the doctor was saying. Her eyes were fixed on Jana, and her vision was coming back. A nurse adjusted the IV trolley, and its castors creaked. The sound brought Nasreen back to the creaking of the trees. And she wondered if, like tinnitus, that eerie sound would haunt her from here on.

She looked at her sister and made another attempt to speak. The nurse held a paper cup of ice water to her lips, and the liquid loosened everything up.

"Jana," Nasreen said, "Where's my phone?"

Jana looked to the nurse, who shrugged, but then said she'd look into it.

"My laptop then," Nasreen said, ignoring the doctor.

"Where is it?" Jana asked.

"My workbag. In my car."

"Your car's probably still parked wherever you left it," she said. "The ambulance brought you in. It might've been towed."

"The office," Nasreen said. "I need to call the office."

Mansour and Emmy came running into the room saying *Yumma* in unison. Nasreen looked past her children, to Jana, repeating once more—this time licking her shriveled lips before she spoke: *I need to call the office.*

Realpolitik

I THOUGHT TALKING POLITICS with the manager at the Salt Cavern would be safe—I mean, salt therapy much? But, turns out, Gary had been held up when he worked as a liquor store cashier and had been backing gun rights legislation by way of NRA donations and bumper sticker activism ever since.

"How about that?" I said. "Awful. Did you put up a fight?"

I slipped off my loafers and slid them under the bench in the waiting room. The bench was upholstered with polar bear pelt, fake.

"God no. I nearly shit my pants!" Gary wears hospital scrubs and, normally, conveys cleanliness and tranquility.

This exclamation, though—this jeopardized the billions of salt micro particles that would be blowing over me for the next forty-five minutes. Fecal matter—I'd be thinking about fucking fecal matter, now. Gary's.

"Interested?" He gestured at the row of Himalayan salt lamps on the shelf behind his desk—pinkish and craggy things.

"I'm good."

"In you go then," he said, rushing me it seemed—he held the door open and everything, something he never does. As though me not wanting to buy a glacier-sized salt lamp with a blank price tag somehow meant our repartee was over.

"Just me today?"

I peered into the empty salt room, which was —appropriately—cavernous.

"Just you," Gary said, nodding, nudging me in.

I prefer the lounger right in front of the aerosol chute—I *really* like to coat myself. I'd be a fool not to take on as many salt crystals as I can. I usually leave with my pants thoroughly salt dusted.

The room is so godsmackingly white, that color palette of peace right down to the polar-bear-on-an-ice-floe bench in the front. And, because the walls, ceiling, and floor are covered with salt gravel, you walk unsteadily in your socks. But once Gary shuts the door, triggers the ionizer, salinizer, and bionic air purifier (it's all *very* scientific, trust me), the room glows blue with ambient light.

What I'd wanted to talk to Gary about—or anyone for that matter—was the toxic sludge that had been dumped up in Ringwood, how heavy metals were showing up in the rivers and the Wanaque Reservoir—I mean, I had *facts*; I was ready to go in on this. But before I could even get it all out, he was all *bang bang, shoot shoot*, talking like, *Those folks need to arm themselves to the teeth!* Talking very *un*-therapeutically, y'know? I couldn't even get out that the people up there already had guns, were hunters, but that it wasn't that sort of a situation. I mean, christ, Gary. A bit quick on the draw, no?

I reclined. I closed my eyes. I tried to clear my mind, alter my mood. Decompress. Breathe. I was ready to be awash in negatively charged salt ions. Heaven, yes.

And in walked Gary, shuffling through salt—his feet in booties and leaving ruts.

Sorry, sorry, sorry, sorry, sorry, he said.

He went to the back row of loungers and bent down. There was a pair of designer sunglasses—big bug-eyed ones—pinched between his fingers as he exited the cavern.

Women (typically jobless housewives with expensive handbags) buddy up on sessions—just another appointment scheduled alongside mani-pedis, lattes, and weekly maintenance visits to the spray tan spa. On the days I get stuck in the cavern with them, it's like pepper spray coming through the aerosol chute. A *kill me now* sort of scenario.

The first time I showed up to the Salt Cavern was because my in-laws gave me a gift certificate for four sessions. Gary handed me a brochure that I read during the session by the light of the EXIT sign. Halotherapy is the impress-the-patron name for salt therapy, *halos* being Greek for salt. But with all his interrupting—and let me tell you, it's happened more than I can ignore—Gary's no refined proprietor, no saint. No halo on Gary. You see what I'm saying?

It wasn't just his retrieving the sunglasses. Five minutes later he was back in the cavern—shuffling his feet through the salt—fiddling with a ceiling vent. I closed my eyes. He coughed a nervous cough as he left. Worse that it was a nervous cough, meaning a cough that didn't have to be coughed. And, I'm fairly certain, he adjusted the volume on the music when he got back to his desk. Knobbed it *down*, then slightly *up*.

Swear to God, I could've killed Gary after the second interruption. I was trying to Zen it up, but my meditation kept slipping from nothingness into somethingness. My mantra of *I am airy* kept mutating into *Die now, Gary.*

My own inability to focus was peeving me. It got serious. I tried to center myself, zeroing in on a single glimmery grain of salt. But...

Intrusive thought: Me palming Gary's skull and slamming it into the wall of the salt cavern. Mineral bits falling loose like the flaking of a popcorn ceiling when the ball hits it. I used to do that intentionally so my little brother's hair would be dandruffed with asbestos.

I tried to center myself, telling myself, *Center, now!* Telling myself, *I am airy.*

Intrusive thought, though: Cutting out early and catching Gary at his desk, the drawstring on his scrubs untied and his waistband slackened to accommodate his stroking hand.

Intrusive thought: Gary's fecal matter. Very tarry.

Relax, I thought to myself. What I was supposed to be doing was relaxing.

It wasn't until "Come As You Are" that I realized the music Gary had been playing over the JBLs was an orchestral rendition of Nirvana's *Nevermind*. C'mon, Gary.

Shit went really wrong when I caught the surveillance

camera in the corner of the salt cavern. One of those orb deals, a black glass bubble with a circle of lights around it. Like the lunar phases poster my brother and I had in our shared bedroom. It was taped to the ceiling and glow-in-the-dark.

There I was having intrusive thoughts about Gary while here, in plain sight, was a reminder that *he* was watching *me*. People sleep in the salt cavern—*I've* slept in the salt cavern. To think Gary's been there the whole time, monitoring, eating a reheated empanada while watching me doze, have hypnic jerks, well on my way down the Eightfold Path. Tell me how that's a fair or appropriate setup.

So Gary got me going, he goaded me, but—*yes*—it was what I did that got me in trouble. Full disclosure: *I* got me going, too—I did.

There was a flicker—*I saw it!* Nobody, neither cop nor shrink, can tell me otherwise. The surveillance camera flickered. Those bioluminescent moons around the bubble did a definite dance.

It was Gary zooming in on me.

I stood up and the lounger went askew. Salt gravel stirred. I crouched down and scraped together fistfuls of salt and flung everything I had with everything I had at the surveillance camera.

My feet kicked the salt gravel, and—admittedly—it pained my toes, even socked. My adrenal glands were working then, and the pain became secondary. I flipped my lounger, then another.

I'm coming out! I belted in the cavern. *Gary, I'm coming out right fucking now!*

Gary opened the door as I barreled through it.

"What's the matter? What happened?" he said.

"You're watching me, Gary! I know what you're up to!"

He backpedaled as I claimed the space behind his desk as my own. And, just as soon as I was mentally present in that space, I outstretched my arms and swept every Himalayan salt lamp off the shelf. The avalanche made a mess at my feet. Some lamps crumbled and big salt clumps chunked off others. I could see inside to the bulbs, the minimal circuitry. Gary dropped to his knees and began to gather the larger parts in his arms like precious gems.

Why why why why why? he said.

"Why, Gary? *Why?*" I said. "Why you shilling for the lamps? Why you watching me while I'm trying to relax, Gary? *Why, why, why?* Don't question me or my actions, Gary. What about the sludge, Gary? THE SLUDGE! Why don't you talk to me about that? You don't care about the people up in Ringwood, Gary? There's toxins in the rivers,

Gary. TOXINS! You're here in your fucking salt tower, you fucking pillar of salt, Gary. You're pure as fuck, Gary. You're a pure soul, aren't you?"

I had moved away from the desk and was standing on the polar bear pelt bench. Gary crawled on his hands and knees behind his desk. That submissive pose made me think I had everything under control, but then again, I wasn't doing much thinking—not of the *critical* variety, anyway. So I was shocked when Gary reemerged at the side of his desk, horizontal on the floor in some action hero position holding a gun with both hands.

"Out!" he said.

And, I'm not ashamed to tell it, all I could say was, *I'm out, I'm out, I'm out.*

I ran through the gently chiming door and crossed the street—death-defyingly—through traffic, still in my socks. I'd swear an oath I could hear the *pock* and *pop* and *kapow* of Gary's gun. I could hear the bullets suck into my skin, an almost sexual sound. The feel of a certain kind of death became apparent when I realized there were three salt therapy sessions remaining on my gift certificate. There was no telling what shape my next encounter with Gary might take.

Super 8

His family is a world to him, and he's the god of that world. So he plans accordingly. The roadside motels with outdoor pools and balconies and railings with beach towels draped over them are too expensive and too NO VACANCY when you book with such short notice. But the kids asked for a vacation, and so he'll bless them with a mini one. (A late god is not an absent god.) Nothing extravagant. They're doing Disney next year, God and tax refund willing, and so even if they deserve more they must settle for less and ration happiness like the sleeve of Ritz crackers they divvy up on the ride down the Parkway.

·

Keansburg has a Super 8 on the highway, and it's reasonably priced and offers a continental breakfast with a waffle maker. The kids love the waffle maker. The waffle maker is a luxury item, even if it does require you to produce the thing yourself prior to consuming it. Their cousins have one on their kitchen counter and put carousel sprinkles in the batter mix when they do slumber parties. Waffle makers—like sprinkles, like sleepovers—are special.

•

But the Super 8 in Keansburg, a mere eighteen minutes and nary a dozen miles from the Sandy Hook beaches, is not the Super 8 they experienced on a trip to Massachusetts summer last. This Super 8 is *sketch*, Yancy says. "Why are you parking in the back lot?" Yancy asks.

"Because that's where our room is," Mac says.

"But it's even scarier back here."

There's no cars in the back, only a dumpster pregnant with trash bags, a pile of unused concrete curb stops, and a wheelbarrow of rebar.

"We should've booked at Red Roof Inn," Yancy says. "Like the one we stayed at for Sesame Place."

"The one with the room that smelled like an ashtray?" Mac asks for clarification. "That one? The one you said smelled like a volcano-sized ashtray?"

"Yes, that one," Yancy confirms.

•

The budget hotel has a definite public health emergency aesthetic. A postindustrial, precarious, heartland-ish aesthetic, despite its location on the Eastern Seaboard. The perfect name for its aesthetic would undoubtedly be *econo-lodge*, so it's a shame that name is trademarked.

•

In front of the building, extending out from the office lobby, is a parking space designated "Vet Parking"—the placard clearly not government-issued. A duo of mangy dogs bite at each other's scruffy necks in the side lot.

The rear entrance, accessible by key card, was propped open with packing tape taped over the latch. A man with a dirty face and the whitest beard was sitting on a curb smoking. A pack of Winstons were squeezed into his shirt pocket.

"Mets, huh?" the man growled, adjusting his body like a bundle of bricks to address Mac's youngest, little Dec Dec. "I can't tell you the number of times I been to Shea."

Mac smiled only because he knew Yancy wouldn't and then used his duffel bag on his shoulder to battering ram little Dec Dec through the door.

"Watch that don't close," the old man said to Mac as he held the door for his wife, his son, and his daughter. Mac gently eased the door closed, careful not to allow it to latch through the packing tape.

•

They arrived at their room on the second floor, and an amoeba-shaped stain—unidentifiable and funkdafied—welcomed them to their temporary residence. As they crossed the threshold, Yancy called it a "tweaker pad" and compared it to an amateur porn film set. Brooke asked, *What's amateur porn?* Yancy commenced a bedbug check, folding down the sheets and flapping the pillowcases.

•

The room tried to pass itself off as fancy, as class. The bathroom smelled like *vomitar*, and the grout around the tub was crust. An infrared heat bulb in the ceiling couldn't make up for those flaws. If anything, it made Mac feel like he was trapped in a reptile tank when he was taking a shit. There was no replacement roll of TP. The sinkside "massage bar," which was just a bar of soap with bumps on it, and faucet water so hard it wouldn't wash the suds from his hands, couldn't suffice either. He wiped his hands on the pilly towel that he dared not press his face to.

Little Dec Dec and Brooke sat side-by-side at the foot of the bed, entranced by the news on CNN as Yancy slapped the back of the remote control in a struggle to make the guide appear on the television screen. The AC unit blew black mold cold over the room, and the mini-fridge, combined with the AC, blended into a prolonged hum.

It was determined and mutually agreed upon that they'd spend as little time as possible in the room, and when they were there, no bare feet on the carpeting was the rule. Yancy closed the back of the remote after rolling the batteries to summon power and shut off the set.

"Let's go to the beach, kids. That's what we're here for, right? Fun!"

•

There was a downpour, with rain dimpling the sand, just as they arrived and purchased their day badges. Mac needed to plead with the badge lady to give him a refund. He and Yancy were allied for once, dead-set against bringing the kids into an arcade, a money pit. They returned to the Super 8 for the indoor pool.

•

This was the summer Brooke took to the water. She was able to dunk her head, raise her fist out of the water, and count five on her fingers before she came up for breath. She did ice cream scoops and frantic kicks enough to resemble swimming, especially when Mac kept his hand under her stomach. She flirted with a dead man's float, occasionally filling her lungs with enough air to keep her body at the surface. Each pool they visited seemed to house its own milestone for Brooke, and the Super 8 was where she had success committing to a jump off the poolside and disappearing her whole self underwater.

"I don't like the look of it," Yancy told Mac. "It's got a sheen."

"A sheen of what?"

"Filth. Molds. I don't know."

"It reeks of chlorine to high heaven. Nothing could survive in that water. Don't worry."

"Overdoing it on the chemicals isn't good either."

"Won't kill them though, Yancy."

"Might turn their blonde heads green, though. Like happened to my sister."

"Really, Yance. Your sister's hair turned green because your mom didn't make you guys shampoo in summer. She said the chlorine water did the cleaning. *You* told me that."

"Still," she said.

•

Mac and Yancy had this joke that only some people got. Yancy got it only after years of courtship with Mac in which she was subjected to watching the Knicks. She liked the sound of Walt Frazier's voice and the look of his suits during the pregame commentary, and she liked Mac's intense frustration watching the team lose. He would pound pillows and punch couch cushions showing no mercy for the stitching holding the furniture together.

So the joke was this: *We can play man-to-man; we can't play zone.* And the joke was this: They wouldn't have any more than two kids, their progeny limited to only Brooke and little Dec Dec. Why, they mused, would any parental unit challenge themselves to being outnumbered by their offspring? That seemed masochistic. It seemed gratuitous.

•

Their defensive efforts came through when it was time for the nightly routine. The children seemed to find second winds, reenergized no-neck monsters. *It's the witching hour*, Yancy would say, almost as an excuse, her patience for the children's misbehavior far exceeding that of Mac's. *No*, Mac would answer, *that's not what that means.*

With the wildcard of a foreign environment—a Super 8 motel swelling with dangers—they struggled to get the kids bed-ready. Little Dec Dec ran laps around the room, hopping over one bed, then the other. He chased Brooke from the bathroom to the window until she turned it around on him. Little Dec Dec, the prey, was quick to tears—incapable of taking what he himself dished out. Sibling stuff. The younger ones never want to be the quarry.

•

The room phone rang.

For someone who doesn't spend extended time in hotels, who doesn't use room service, who doesn't order escorts, who doesn't arrange drug deals, weapons smuggling, or human trafficking, there's really no good reason that statement should be uttered. But it happened.

The room phone rang, and it might be more accurate to say, "The room *telephone* rang," because the Super 8 room phone was antiquated. It had a coiled cord and buttons that actually need pressing.

Everyone stopped when the ringing started. "Pick it up," Yancy said, little Dec Dec in her clutches. And Mac did. Reluctantly, he held the phone to his ear because, well, germs.

"Hello?"

Stop that stomping.

"Sorry?"

Stop stomping. You're stomping on my ceiling. I'm trying to sleep.

"Stomping?"

I'm in the room below you. I'm trying to sleep.

"Alright," Mac said. "No problem."

He heard the click of the other phone, upset that he didn't beat the man to the hang-up.

Mac was immediately irritated at how the exchange had gone. *Here's a guy*, Mac figured, who's going to complain about the soft pitter-patter of my children's feet, and not even eight o'clock in the evening yet? The kids hadn't even been running around like that for five minutes. *Here's a guy*, Mac continued to calculate, who knows the lay of the hotel well enough to know the room number directly above him? Is that a common knowledge sort of thing? This must not be his first noise complaint, Mac guessed. And these thoughts piled one on top of the other until they filled him with a swelling sense of indignation. *How, the fuck, could this guy be so presumptuous as to call our room?*

•

Mac would've moved quickly to resolve this issue—in his mind, it had become an issue—if the guy's voice had been different, less sinister. The guy sounded groggy (so maybe he was asleep or pilled-out), and croakish, and crackish. Maybe there was a meth lab operation downstairs. Just propane tanks in the tub, Sudafed foils on the sink, coffee filters and glass cookware scattered across the floor. Mac thought of his family exploding into body part bits as the floor blew up beneath them. He stopped hesitating.

Yancy lowered little Dec Dec into the tub. Mac poked his head into the bathroom and told Yancy he'd be back in a few.

"You're not going down there, are you Mac?"

"Don't worry about it," he said.

"Look at that," he added, pointing to the upper corner of the bathtub, then the opposite corner. There was what looked like a stainless steel button on one side and a piece of hardware on the other. Yancy pulled on the button to satisfy her husband's curiosity—a retractable clothesline.

"Easy suicide access," Mac said.

"Kids!" Yancy said.

•

Mac smelled the chlorine, strong, as the elevator doors opened to the first floor. He passed the lobby and tried to appear casual. *Should've brought the empty ice bucket along*, he thought. Always walk with purpose.

He knocked on the door and nobody answered. He didn't want to lean his ear to it because he could imagine a person on the other side with an eye to the peephole.

He knocked again and still nothing. He felt embarrassed but relieved. It was the relief of a non-issue. It was mundanity.

But then there was the thud of the latch arm, and a rustling, and the door opened.

A girl no older than Brooke stood in the doorway. She wore a grown man's undershirt that touched her wrists and shins. Her feet were bare and her blonde hair was shoulder-length, oily and stringy and green-tinged. Her eyebrows were thick and darker than the hair on her head. Those eyebrows and the gap in her teeth were what would get her stopped in a mall corridor in a few short years and asked if she's ever considered a modeling career. She was holding an iPad at her waist, and the glow of it lit her up. She could've been Brooke if not for the green in her hair.

Mac looked beyond the girl to the hotel room that framed her. Yes, it was identical to his room on the second floor, just as it was identical to thousands of other hotel rooms around the country, but this one was markedly different.

Three boxes of Brisk iced tea cans were stacked next to the bathroom door. There was a tower of plastic totes beside those, with yellow Shop Rite bags spilling from the lids. Mac saw the dull shimmer of a scattered pile of soda can tabs on the dresser. He eyed the diamond sides of a drying rack with clothes draped over it—pant legs like a man exhausted. Orange extension cords squiggled across the floor forming a crossroads of wires and power strips. There was junk everywhere. A wrinkled McDonald's bag was on the bedspread. Wawa coffee cups were abandoned on the hard carpeting. Cereal boxes were arranged, neatly actually, right inside the doorway. Sandals and work boots right beside them. It was difficult for Mac to focus through the clutter.

The ironing board for the room was functioning

as a tabletop with a lamp on it, miscellaneous papers with three-folds and torn envelopes, too. My Little Pony figures were lined up along the edge. A bath towel was laid out in the entranceway as a welcome mat. The office chair was pushed beside the back window where extra pillows and hotel linens and more than a few stuffed animals were heaped. The shades were drawn so no outside light, be it moon-light or streetlight, got in. A box fan was on the floor, and a laundry basket, too—its handles were broken. The TV was on, blaring something with crowd noise, and Mac saw two tube-socked feet crossed at the ankles on the bedspread.

"Can I talk to your dad?" Mac asked the girl. Without taking her eyes from the iPad screen, she spun around and threw herself onto the bed.

•

The dad, in retrospect, was what was to be expected. His greasy hair was matted down from hours under a hat. His t-shirt was sleeveless, but his arms were unre-markable. Safe to say the guy hadn't done a pushup in years. Still, he approached with confidence, fearlessness, as though his bare feet, jean shorts, and puffy eyes were images of intimidation.

"What do you want?" he asked, the croaky voice now unfiltered by phone hiss.

"I wanted to know why you called my room."

Mac fucked up, in that he stammered.

The dad needed to take a moment to register what was said. He seemed genuinely shocked Mac would show up at his door. Genuinely shocked that Mac was the guy from upstairs. But when that shock subsided, the dad came at the encounter differently.

"Because you were stomping on the fucking floor!"

Whatever pluck Mac had arrived at the door with was sapped from his entire demeanor when the dad came at him like that.

"I've got two little kids…" Mac started.

"I don't give a fuck. Get control of them then. You don't see my daughter jumping up and down like a fucking maniac disturbing the place."

"They weren't jumping," Mac answered defensively.

"Well I don't know what the fuck they were doing then. Bang, bang, banging on my ceiling while I'm trying to rest. While my daughter is trying to rest. Take some fucking responsibility, guy!"

"Your daughter's on her video game," Mac said, pointing to the green-haired girl sitting on the foot of the bed, unbothered by the scene at the door.

"Are you trying to drag my daughter into this, asshole?" The dad stepped through the threshold of the door.

"I'm just pointing out…"

"You better step the fuck off, brother."

The dad came as close as kissing to Mac.

"Chill out," Mac said, and then the dad pushed him backwards, forceful enough that Mac staggered.

"Stay the fuck away from my door," the dad leveled. He backed into his room and let the door close.

•

Mac walked the corridor past the pool and toward the back of the hotel, exiting through the same rear entrance they'd entered through earlier. The curb-smoker was gone, and with him, the packing tape latch rig. Mac patted his pockets, realizing he didn't have his key card, as the door locked behind him.

He sat on the curb and looked at his phone.

Is everything alright???

Mac answered Yancy's text with *all good* and *be back in a few*. He walked across the empty parking lot toward the highway intersection.

There was a homeless man standing on the median, panhandling. There was a bucket between his feet. He was holding a sign up to the cars that caught the red. *Please give it too me*, the sign said. There was either a Celtic cross or a Venus symbol on the sign, too. The drawing was sloppy, and Mac couldn't figure which. Mac watched the homeless man approach car windows based on whether they were open or not. He watched one woman in her car sitting deathly still, careful not to move and risk being misread as someone searching for spare change.

•

Mac retraced his steps back to the hotel parking lot. He entered through the main lobby.

The continental breakfast was already set up. Sure, there was Saran wrap over the mini-bagels and white bread slices, lids on the ice buckets where the yogurts were stored, and milk cartons were still refrigerated. But seeing the whole setup there at nine o'clock in the evening belied the hotel's claim of *freshness*. The bananas in the fruit bowl were already browning.

"Do you mind if I make a waffle?" Mac asked the receptionist. She was sleepy, stoned maybe, and too young an employee to police the food, Mac thought.

"We're not supposed to let people take food until the morning shift," she said.

"Who's *we?*" Mac asked.

She looked around and seemed to understand his point.

"Okay," she said. "Whatever. The batter is in the mini-fridge."

Mac removed four cups of batter from the mini-fridge and lined them up on the counter. He clicked on the waffle maker and admired the red glow of the switch. He poured the batter into the machine, watching

the lumpy batter flow into each of the channels and res-
ervoirs of the circle. Once evenly spread, he closed the
lid, flipped the machine, and watched the digital display
count down. He went through this process three more
times.

Mac grabbed a styrofoam plate and stacked up the
waffles. He shoved a safe number of syrup packets and
utensils into his pockets. He intended to say thanks to
the receptionist, but now he felt the enterprise had a
strong stealing vibe, so he just slinked past her.

•

Mac knocked on the door with his knee. Yancy, Brooke,
and little Dec Dec all answered, competing for space in
the doorway.

Where were you, Dad? the kids asked, whining.
They were in their pajamas now, bathed and ready for
bed. Yancy had even allowed them to go barefoot. She
guided them back into the room and took the plate
from Mac.

"What happened? Everything okay?"

"Yeah, everything's fine," Mac told her.

Mac couldn't *not* think about his footfalls on the
hotel room floor. He couldn't *not* think about the excite-
ment he generated in his children by showing up with
the waffles stacked and steaming on a single plate.

"Look what your father brought, kids. How did

he even do that?" she asked, asking them, but really asking him.

"I've got a lot of influence around this hotel," Mac said.

They gathered around the hotel room dresser as Yancy cut the waffles into pieces. Mac passed around forks and peeled back the lids on the syrup packets. They all stood, feasting on the breakfast, starving from the day. It was a dessert, a treat, for his entire family.

Mass Surveillance

Our apartment is modest—by which I mean small, lacking privacy. I don't mean to say the place demurs and says things like, "Oh, it's nothing." It's small, but the walls are thick, concrete, damn near soundproof. So when our second child—Kid 2, if I'm speaking to you with acquaintance informality—barks a cough, I barely hear it. It's muffled. Like either I've got a pillow over my ears, or she's got a pillow over her face, which—I think we can all agree—wouldn't be good.

·

A *bark*, that's how everyone describes the croup cough. The internet, the pediatrician, my mother-in-law who used to sit with the infant-version of my wife in the bathroom, the shower running hot. The steam opens up the airways, she says, the bronchi. *You should try it.* I usually make a dismissive sound with my mouth when she shares these home remedies with me, but in this case, the pediatrician agreed it could be effective. He also said, thanks to the steroid, the cough should clear in another day, or at least morph into something less canine. So I stay out of the steamy bathroom with Kid 2. It's something I'd really rather not do.

·

Our bed—modest, too (size-wise, again)—used to be something we described to other couples to indicate our closeness, our intimacy. "I'll go no bigger than a full," my wife would say. "If you're not touching your spouse while you sleep, why even be married?" I never actually agreed, just nodded along automaton-style. I've always been bothered by lifeless limbs touching mine and the sour and stale mucosa of sleeping breath. I never said this, of course, but I can't say I'm not a little pleased of late that she's been curled up at her side—her edge—as far from me as possible.

·

Of late. Since I forgot to flush my dip, I mean. It would only be right for me to quit smoking along with her. That was the case she made when Kid 2 was gestating. Fair enough, I thought. But why I wasn't allowed to chew, I didn't get that. So there she went—middle of the night bladder works—lifted the seat and saw my unflushed amber-brown globule of chewed chewing tobacco floating there. And I've been sleeping untouched ever since.

•

I had Kid 1 on his back in an open field once. Struggling with him, *really* struggling. He was squirming, his legs kicked, back arched like a stone bridge, and he squealed, too. A jogger cut across the grass and ran full speed toward us, shouting incoherently and flailing. He sure as hell wasn't jogging. *Stop that, stop that!* I didn't know what he was on about, so when he arrived at us I just stared, gripping Kid 1's ankles in one hand and smearing clean the shit from his butt cheeks with the other. *Sorry*, the man said. *I thought you were hurting him.* And he just walked off. *Were you?* my wife asked when I told her the story. Then it was my turn to walk off.

•

I've confessed to my wife that sometimes, while she sleeps, I masturbate in bed. *Don't do that*, she said.

•

Now when I rub one out I tiptoe into the bathroom, mock taking a dump, and hunch my back and do it right into the toilet. No fuss; no cleanup. Nice and easy. I flush. You bet your ass I flush. I always remember to flush now. I'm the fucking mayor of Flushing, Queens.

•

Kid 2 soothes herself by twining many strands of hair around the nipple of her paci. She was born with a full head of hair, which—I learned—is something people like to comment on. The nurse in the maternity ward mohawked her hair, which I thought a good look to offset the austere plexiglass of the hospital bassinets.

Everyone raved, and everyone's a know-it-all where babies are concerned. So it was all, *What a head of hair! Too bad it's gonna fall out.* It didn't, thank you very much. And Kid 2 has always—as soon as it was reachable— twined that hair around the nipple of her paci. On the monitor, you can hear the *puck puck puck* of her suckling mouth. Clear as day.

In the mornings it's a project. You've got to extricate the nipple from her mouth and her hair from the nipple. It's easy, sometimes, like unraveling a spool of thread. But there are days where it's a mess—a matted, knotted mess of hard and soft, old and fresh, saliva and stringy hair. Those days, when a comb won't even go through it, I need to cut it. It would be bad news if she did, so it's good my wife never notices.

•

At five one spring morning I bounded out of bed, slid up the window screen, and punched and hissed at the birds in the apricot tree squawking in jovial mating or good worm breakfast—if I'm being honest, I don't know what the hell they were doing. And my wife told this story for months after: how I was asleep, in some state of hysterical somnolence, trying to shush birds. For one, I *wasn't* sleeping. The point was I had been awakened. For another, why does she think interrupting birds' breakfast or nut-busting in an effort to silence them is so absurd? These things about her bother me. I find them bothersome.

•

We have two video cameras—each perched on a curtain rod and angled down. One watches Kid 1 in his bed; the other watches Kid 2 in her crib. And I watch the monitor as much as I can. The monitor scans from CAM 1 to CAM 2 in eight-second intervals. I refer to this as our surveillance state. My wife doesn't like my fixation on the monitor screen. She thinks it's what's made me such an absent husband. Better than an absent father, though. No? I mean if she had to pick one…

•

The monitor scans from CAM 1 to CAM 2, from Kid 1 to Kid 2. Barking Kid 2 is apparent, loud, while Kid 1 slumbers silently, and all I can hear through the monitor is the white noise machine hissing. These are the sounds that keep me up.

Kid 1 wasn't always so easy. Kid 1 had a feeding tube from birth—a motility disorder, gastrointestinal complications. I've heard my wife say these terms innumerable times to family and friends, updating them on our child's health. He's on the spectrum, too, so we're hamstrung by all these early intervention appointments, therapies, and so forth. I don't mean to sound unconcerned, I don't. But he had water on the brain, too. Sympathize with me. They call it hydrocephalus. It made his head larger than it should be. It didn't stay that way, but at the time I couldn't stop thinking of the Elephant Man. I thought about what it would be like to be the father to the Elephant Man.

•

My wife cops a 'tude when she stirs and sees me awake in bed with my eyes glued to the monitor screen. I even hold it in my hands on my chest like it's a Game Boy or something (I'm aging myself now). She's always harping, nitpicking. It's been this way, especially since the chewing tobacco incident.

One morning in our past, pre-children life, I woke and looked out our apartment window. Below was a scene of clementines spilled from their box. The pattern in which they had spread over the cracked slabs of beige sidewalk was a thing of natural beauty. So, natch, I unhooked my Canon AE-1 from the doornail on which it hung and took a photo, my body daredevilishly angling out the window. "You're gay," my wife said when she realized what I was doing. I should've taken that as a warning sign, I guess. Not that I was gay, because I'm not; but that she was a nag, because she is.

•

Last week I watched a Filipino couple walking to church and the smell of the woman's perfume wafted in my direction. It made me think of the few times my wife dabbed some fragrance behind her earlobes, between her breasts. Like when her ma got remarried and my wife had to wear these ridiculous elbow-length gloves, like a debutante or something. She was the maid-of-honor. If you knew my wife, you'd know how out of character the look was.

Arriving back at our modest apartment later that night—the apartment when it still had an office space and not a nursery—we both, a bit drunk and wired from the obligatory foolish dancing, made love. She kept the debutante gloves on, and I kept my tie around my neck, per her instructions. We don't play like that anymore, though. Insert a dad joke about BDSM here.

•

Sleep's been awful. They say once you've got kids you'll never sleep the same again, soundly. I admit I think they're right. I wake at the randomest hours and for no conceivable reasons. I'm doomed if I don't fall back to sleep within five minutes. When that happens, I stagger stiffly to the courtyard outside and sit on a step beside the clusterbox. The other day I was doing this and saw a man run by buck-ass naked with only a tie loosened around his neck. I thought that might've been me from my not-so-distant past. Honest. Like it was the universe trying to tell me something, knowing a streaker would get my attention.

•

I hear Kid 2 cough through the walls and then through the monitor. Through my sleep haze, I wonder if we could call the cough a bark. The croup should have cleared up by now.

I sit up in bed, open my laptop, and see a Facebook post by my sister. She's given birth to her second child, her Kid 2. She's an anti-vaxxer who lives, inconceivably, in the Maldives. We're estranged. I copy and paste the post, an ecstatic birth announcement, into a Word document for safekeeping. It's too good not to save.

> *On September 2, on the same day as the world experienced the cosmic energy of a solar eclipse and the magical new beginnings of a Virgo new moon, we welcomed our second little daughter into this world and our lives. She came peacefully during a gentle rainstorm at 11:43 in the*

evening, born into the water at home after four hours of labor. She weighed in at 8lbs even and 19 inches long. She is beautiful, perfect, healthy and loved beyond belief. I'm so infinitely grateful for another beautiful birth experience, and another strong, healthy Virgo daughter. A huge shout out to my kick ass midwife Lexi Stephenson of Blossoming Waterbirth who came to the Maldives and supported and helped me to have exactly the birth I wanted with such strength and grace. Baby has not found her name yet, but mom and dad and her sister are working on it and know that the perfect name will soon come to this sweet angel. In the meantime we just call her Sister.

#babysister #rootedinlove #eclipsebaby #newmoonblessings #waterbirth #homebirth #soinlove #growingfam #thentherewere4

I sort of envy her ignorance, her faith. I envy her living on an island, even if it will be submerged by the sea most likely in seconds. I wish our apartment and bed were bigger. I wish we had a waterbed. This modesty hasn't gotten us anywhere as a couple.

•

My wife doesn't know this, but when Kid 2's locks get

tangled around the paci nipple, and the only means of releasing her from the hair prison of her own making is the scissors, I secret the hardened sections of hair into sandwich bags. I seal them. I've got Ziplocs of the stuff. For lockets, I figure. Sometime down the line. It's an imagining I have, of the wife and me in a spacious suburban home with a California king, her head resting on my lifting chest, and no sleep interruptions but the rustle of expensive sheets—percale ones. Then and only then I'll reveal the Ziplocs of baby hair, and I'll place them between my wife's bare breasts as she reclines in bed, and I'll say to her, *See, honey. See how very far we've come.*

Ariana Grande

We were balling it up no less than three days a week at the Wayne PAL when, I guess, Jer tired of me complaining about being broke. The PAL (that's "Pigs Always Lurking," for the uninitiated) charges a five dollar entry fee to the gym, which to me is a joke when I start thinking about civil asset forfeiture and how the courts there are no less sticky-sweaty than the courts at the park. But nobody plays at the park, so I bum the five bucks from Jer.

He said he had work for me, that I could join his "team" of driveway sealcoaters, his uncle's operation in the summer season. I was like *nah* at first, but because purchasing a 40-ounce of malt liquor had become something of a financial hardship, I took him up on the offer.

My mom called it an "apprenticeship" on the phone with my aunt, but that made the job sound way more involved and skilled than it really was. The only training it required was for me to watch Jer and our other boy Amaury do it a few times before I started to follow their lead.

Our team was three, and Jer's uncle called us the Three Stooges, whose work none of us were familiar with, but when we returned Uncle Hugh's pickup at the end of each day he shook our hands while repeating "Success!"

There's that.

There's also the blue shirts Jer's uncle gave us to wear which said *Grabowski Paving and Sealcoating* across the back. Jer's got that *-ski* ending to his name, but I'm the Polack of the group. Jer's just white, I guess—mongrel something or other. Amaury's a Dominicano, but—unlike other dudes from DR I know—rarely mentions it. We call Jer's uncle—the bossman, that is—*Grab-ass-ski*, because how could we not?

As much as I cherish hearing Uncle Hugh wish us well in the morning as we load our teenage selves into his truck in the driveway of his slightly-larger-than-mine home, Jer did not make it clear to me we'd be on the hook for working Saturdays. Even Uncle Hugh's brilliant pronunciation of asphalt (he pronounces it *ash-phalt*) can't compensate for my weekend time. It's like, I thought everybody was working for the weekend, right motherfucker?

The ride is a beat-to-shit, late-'90s Tacoma with a carry-on trailer hitched to the back. The polypropylene tank's set there and all the buckets and brooms and other equipment we need, too. We pile into the cab—I'm squished sitting bitch seeing as how I'm the new guy— and Uncle Hugh smacks the hood and shouts *Neat and clean and even lines!* at us, which is clearly his mantra and what would close out his TV ad if he ever had one. The license plate hanging by a zip-tie off the back gate of the trailer scrapes and sparks as it drags down the street.

Jer—one year me and Amaury's senior and already with a driver's license—has us rumbling and rattling through town—it's a well-potholed city, the roads still decimated from the snowplows—and it's already sweaty. I knew it when the seat of my pants failed to slide across the leather interior. We've been heatwaving for days now, and weatherman says it shows no signs of relenting.

I scratch my head which is freshly shaved for summer and even more freshly lotioned with a sunscreen that's seriously five years, if not more, expired. So it lathered on thick, and it took mad rubbing before I even appeared like a person—not a ghost—again. When I scratch my head there are slivers of white beneath my fingernails: coagulated sunscreen—it's like Elmer's glue. It's so thick I trust it will block the sun. I'm calling bullshit on expiration dates.

This ain't the business to be in if you're no good in the hotness. But here I am.

Our first stop is on the rich side of town, the hilly Heights side (always with the *actual* physical superiority of well-off families, right?), but with a relatively basic driveway considering those cigar-chewing, snobby types tend to splurge on absurd designs and paving options. Showing-off, I get it. I'd probably do the same. I'd definitely have a fancy-ass Roman fountain in my front yard landscaping if I had the cash. Believe that.

But this homeowner keeps it simple.

He's not home, mind you. Nobody is. I don't know anything about him or the missus or their offspring, if they have any. We're here, entrusted to act honorably and responsibly, on his property and in his absence. Model citizens, yes indeedy.

The three of us stooges work at a pace we've all nonverbally agreed on. We've got a smooth rotation going, too. So no one of us is ever doing all the heavy lifting. We take turns, house to house, with the duties of the job.

Rolling up to this house—yes, it's got the Everyman's straightaway driveway, but it's also flexing with decorative bushes that look like bonsai trees, the kinds you can only get at tree nurseries or some such place (I really don't know) that specialize in such unnatural looking designs—we're not even through letting down the gate on the trailer before a little girl from next-door sets upon us like a pigtailed fly on roadkill.

Not the first time this has happened. Kids, I've learned in all my teenage wisdom, like to watch people do shit. Okay, I'll revise to say they like to watch people do shit they haven't seen before. Especially some dudes who are typically balling hard in a gym or gaming in their jerkoff lairs. Kids, it seems, have a thing for watching labors get carried out. Bless their innocent souls.

We go about our business, though—professionals that we are—unloading the supplies onto the sidewalk. Amaury is all serious-faced as he gets a jump on clearing the debris and aggregate from the driveway using the gas-powered leaf blower. The little girl inches closer to the property line—her family's driveway parallels this one. Jer uses the stiff brush, following Amaury's path, to get rid of whatever remains after he blows. It's gotta be done like this. Jer, by way of the distinguished Uncle Hugh, insists the driveway needs to be free of any substance. You want the sealcoat applied as smooth as your girlfriend's ass, he says. I don't have a girlfriend. Many thanks to my impoverished high school social life.

If I'm being forthright, I'm not personally doing much. I prep the coal tar emulsion, which is the concoction—the secret sauce—we've got stashed in the polypropylene tank. But that don't take much. Hook up the hose. Drag it into position. Amaury and Jer are still prepping. Amaury hot lances the cracks while Jer takes up a weedwacker and has his way with the crabgrass sprouting from the edges of the driveway. I'm not being lazy, it's just we've got this rotation I mentioned. I lucked out in that I was the lead man on the last job. And that job was yesterday. So I'm shovel-leaner on this sweltering Saturday morning. Praise be to Allah, Jah, and Jesus. And I can pick the calluses at the base of my fingers without a worry of my fellow workers giving me trouble. We're good like that, copacetic.

The little girl's doing the kid stare thing. The thing where they lack the social maturity to realize staring at someone, all but unblinking, is a rude fucking way to interact in public. Because I'm such a proper young gentleman, and because she's beginning to freak me out, I dab to try to elicit a reaction.

Nothing.

"Fill those cracks," Amaury tells me. He finishes blowing, and Uncle Hugh's instructions clearly state equipment needs to be returned to the trailer as its use is done with, so Amaury bungees the leaf blower back into place on the trailer. "You need the new jug," he says of the crack filler. "It's in the cab." I fetch it like a good employee and crouch to do what needs doing. There's a few patches of alligatored pavement to get to, and my thighs start burning before long. It's like doing defensive stance drills, shuffling from baseline to midcourt and back during tryouts each Thanksgiving weekend. That burn is only intensified from the sun beating back up at me off the black asphalt, too. I repeat *neat and clean* under my labored breath as I try to keep the jug steady.

Amaury and Jer ditch their Nikes for these special rubber boots—"tar walkers," we call them—as I finish up. Then they start filling buckets at the tank and carrying them to the far end of the driveway. I've got the downtime, so instead of just gesturing, I engage the little girl verbally.

I ask if she plays *Fortnite*. She shakes her head no.

I ask if she plays *Minecraft*. No, she shakes. Then she adds (so at least now I'm more confident she's not on the spectrum or something): "But my cousin does."

That workhorse Amaury starts squeegeeing the driveway. Jer's in charge of spilling the emulsion from the buckets every minute or so, whenever the stuff's spread just as it should be. Bossman Grab-ass-ski demands we push and pull the squeegee at least three times, but we never do more than twice. One time the sealer didn't bond and Uncle Hugh flipped the fuck out on us, threatened to fire us—even Jer, his own nephew— but I figured he was more inclined to pummel us. He's that type. *Old school*, they say, which I've always taken as code for abusive.

Nothing this little girl has ever experienced, that's for sure. Not unless her daddy's some agro alcoholic after dark, which, I mean, he *could* be. She disappears as we're in the monotonous part of the job now, but also the most mesmerizing—Amaury spreading that stuff in some percussion-heavy island rhythm. I beatbox the beat I've got in my head to him.

"Like that, right Amaury?"

"Shut up, Lukas," he tells me. No respect.

The little girl reemerges, so my guess that the tarry stench sitting in the air wasn't what drove her away. No, she's back with a basketball now—not even a youth ball either—and so I know we're in for some stranger bonding. I'm actually not that on-point when it comes to balling, but I compensate by doing an unnecessary amount of fancy dribbling on offense and hounding cats on D. The whole gym hates me.

"You play basketball?" I ask her. She's dribbling well for a five-year-old, or however old she is.

"Yeah."

"You practice dribbling a lot?"

"With my fingertips," she says. Fundamentals, of course.

"Who's your favorite player?"

She comes out with "Michael Jordan," which tells me she's got a dad who rips on Lebron and KD and probably Curry, too. He probably calls them soft in front of her. Tells her the game is different from what it used to be.

"I'm Michael Jordan's trainer," I tell her. She smiles but doesn't laugh. I'm not that funny.

"No," she says.

"I am," I say. "I'm his trainer. I taught him every thing he knows."

Amaury nears the end of the driveway. Jer spills one more batch of emulsion onto the ground and carries the bucket back to the trailer. Bungees it securely. It splashes. The whole truck, mind you, is black spattered with emulsion.

"Michael Jordan is 55."

So now I know shorty's dad is an obsessive. He's

probably got Concords on pedestals in his study. He's probably got authenticated jerseys with the league insignia embroidered on and shit. He might even have the Fleer rookie card behind glass on the wall next to his postgrad diplomas and wedding pictures with wifey. Depends on how well-off dude is.

"I'm 56," I tell her.

"No, you're not."

"I am. I'm 56 and I'm his trainer. I taught him everything he knows," I say again. She sees through me, and not just because I'm Powder pale.

She dribbles through her legs—not well. She lifts the leg so the ball can have passage through. Still, impressive for her age.

Amaury finishes up the driveway and he and Jer douse their shirts with the garden house on our customer's house. They wrap the sopping shirts around their necks to stay cool.

With the driveway complete, sealcoated to perfection—if I do say so myself (it's neat and clean with even lines, for sure)—we gradually pack the equipment onto the trailer. There's no rush, because Uncle Hugh demands we stick around until the sealcoat "settles." He stresses that sometimes the emulsion sinks into the cracks we haven't filled well enough. Wait five, ten minutes after the job, he says. In the meantime, Amaury fetches two pine stakes, a mallet, and a roll of yellow caution tape from the cab.

"I'm kind of a big deal," I tell the little girl. "I'm surprised you haven't heard of me before. You've heard of Michael Jordan but not the guy who taught him everything he knows? That's strange."

"You are not 56," she says, assertive now. Her tone has changed. She's comfortable, I can tell. Not nervous to raise her voice to a teenager.

"I am 56," I say. "I'm an old person."

"You're *not*." She throws her head back and lets out a groan. About done with me, I guess. Or maybe just hamming it up the way kids are prone to.

"Ask him." I point to Amaury. He's hammering the two stakes into the grass strips that run alongside the driveway. "He's brown," I say. "So you know he tells the truth. Brown people always tell the truth. I'm 56, ain't I Amaury?"

He nods unconvincingly, and he's smiling too, which doesn't help my case. Jer ties the caution tape to one stake in a fine shoelace bow, and Amaury does the same on the other side.

"I'm an old person," I say. "I'm a great-grandma."

"You'd be a grand*pa*."

"Whoa! It's 2019. Don't you know that? You better watch what you say."

I've got Amaury and Jer smirking now. They're entertained. The job is done, no sealcoat is sinking, and their necks and backs are dripping cool.

A guy in his own pickup truck double-parks next to ours. I can tell from the way his arm hangs out the window that he's here to haggle. He hops out. He's small, and probably short-dicked, so we know why he's overcompensating with the vehicle. There're oversized tires on the truck, too, with treads so big I could nap in them. That's a dead giveaway on the cock-size as well. He staggers Napoleonically toward us at the end of the driveway, our masterwork.

"How much you guys charging for that?" he asks.

"350," Jer tells him.

"Bullshit," he says. "C'mon. Right now. Do my driveway. I'm around the block. $300."

"Not a chance," Jer says. Jer's pretty quiet, but he can talk to adults like he's channeling his Uncle Hugh. It's the Grab-ass-ski bravado. Business acumen. They con— they don't get conned.

"C'mon," the guy says. "I'll pay cash money right now. $300."

Jer motions to Amaury and they close the gate on the trailer, lock it up, make it appear as if we're out, though I know we've still got a minute or two left on the waiting clock for the sealcoat.

"$325," he says, hand extended.

"$340," Jer says. "I can't go any less. This is the top-of-the-line emulsion we got here." He smacks his hand on the polypropylene tank. "Coal tar. You won't need another visit from us for three years minimum."

"Okay, $340," he says. "I'm right around the corner. I'll be out there."

"We'll be around after this," Jer says. They shake hands and he speeds off as though we might beat him there. His truck gurgles.

"You see that?" I ask.

"See what?" the little girl asks back. She was watching, enraptured as far as I could tell, the interaction between our next customer and Jer.

"We just made 340 more dollars."

She doesn't respond. She dribbles. The ball bounces off her foot and rolls into the street. She runs after it but stops at the curb. Well-trained. Her dad's definitely a hard-ass. Amaury races into the road and scoops up the ball. "Throw me the rock," I yell to him. He does, and I do a crossover and gently hand the ball back to her. Jer bitches about how close I am to the driveway.

"You see these moves?"

"Yeah."

"These are the moves that trained the greatest player to ever do it."

"Michael Jordan," she says.

"You got it! MJ! I'm rich," I tell her. "I get paid one dollar to do this." I wave my hand magically over the driveway. "I'm a millionaire. I've got three houses. I'm a rich man. Michael Jordan made sure of it."

"What's your name?"

"My name? You want to know my name?" I turn to Amaury and Jer. They're sitting in the cab with the doors open, trading a jug of Arnold Palmer back and forth. I never take my share because Jer's backwash is fucking gross. "She wants to know my name, guys. I'm Julius Erving."

She doesn't react.

"What's your name?" I ask.

"Ariana."

"Like Ariana Grande."

"Who's that?"

"Guys," I yell to the guys. They're not paying me any mind, though. They're laughing about something, passing and swigging from that Arnold Palmer jug. They might as well be making out. "This is Ariana Grande over here."

"I bet you can't dunk it," Ariana says. Now, since we've gotten personal I guess, she's all about challenging me. Of course, I can't dunk. But what can a five-year-old know about heights and palming and adjustable hoops.

"Watch this," I tell her. I stand still. "See that?"

"See what?"

"I just dunked it."

"No you didn't."

"Yes I did. Watch." I stand still some more. "I just dunked it again."

"You did not," Ariana says.

"I did. It was so quick you didn't even see it. I rushed over to you, stole the ball from your hands, ran down your driveway, and slammed it into your hoop, and returned it to your hands."

"That's impossible."

"Nothing's impossible," I tell her, feeling like a motivational speaker as I say it.

"You can't dunk it," Ariana says again, seemingly certain of my shortcomings as a player when it comes to vertical leaps.

"All this dunking has me exhausted," I say, and I walk over to Amaury and Jer sitting in the cab. They're all laughs as I approach. Ariana dribbles the ball, following my path toward the truck. "Careful not to let the ball roll into your neighbor's driveway," I say.

"What the fuck you two laughing about over here?" I say to Amaury and Jer as I swipe the Arnold Palmer from Amaury's hands. And I instantly see what. Jer's at the steering wheel with his legs spread and his mesh shorts yanked down. He's got the yellow caution tape wrapped several times around his half-erect dick. I nearly shit. Jer keeps unraveling the roll, and his tip looks nothing short of strangled. It's only when we're all laughing at the same time, increasingly louder, that I turn to my left and see Ariana standing right beside me. She's holding the ball like a hug to her belly, and I breathe out an *Oh shit*. Amaury sees her too, and he elbows Jer hard in the arm. He quickly pulls the waistband on his shorts back up.

I close the passenger side door only to open it again. I need to get in.

"Nice talking to you," I say to Ariana, and I'm still unsure of what she's seen. I push Amaury over to the middle of the cab and slam the door shut. We pull away and the license plate on the trailer scrapes and sparks against the gravel. It's rough-sounding, guttural as hell. I lean forward and look in the sideview. I see Ariana, getting smaller by the second as Jer speeds up. She's dribbling the ball back toward her house just as she should, nothing but her fingertips doing the work.

The Bleeding Lodge

MIDDY'S MOM HAD NEGLECTED her roots for years. "They live in the hills," she said of her native relations, "and I live in Paterson, and that's that." Middy never asked about it—*what was there to ask?* The most she'd known of Indians was Sacagawea, forget about knowing kin. For all she knew, she was just another girl in the seventh grade at New Roberto Clemente. Eighth grade come September. She had to suffer through a trio of novels for summer reading, complicated by her reject prescription glasses, which were all blurry spots and eyestrains. "Christmas," her mom said. "Just squint harder until Christmas."

But then Middy's mom got wrangled by her estranged sister Ruthie at a viewing. Ruthie told her, "Lottie, when are you going to come visit? Don't you miss the trees, the milkweed, Orrin's fiddle music?"

"You mean mosquitoes, police murder, and white neighbors throwing dog shit at my doorstep? That what you mean?"

"You know that's only the half," Ruthie said. "You talk like Paterson is some prize."

"Well, I don't miss it any," Lottie said.

She walked away from her nettling sister and clapped two brass praying hands around an envelope containing her sympathy card for the deceased. Ruthie shuffled up behind her.

"We're having a powwow later this month," Ruthie told her. And though Lottie's initial take was to tell Ruthie to forget about it, to fuck off, she looked at the body in the casket across the room, thought of the elders who once taught her whittling and the ocarina whistle when she was a youngblood, and said, *Okay, I'll be there.*

She left Middy and kid brother with a neighbor and drove north to a fairground just outside Ringwood State Park. She watched a jingle dancer perform for the powwow crowd, and it was like a garden hose slacked into an oil tank and sucked at on the open end—she was siphoned back into that native world she'd long forsaken and labeled as foolish.

That same day Lottie returned to Paterson and collected empty snuff tins from the geezers who sat on crates outside the corner bodega, packratting until she could heft them to the Tribal Center as a donation. An elder took them from her, said *Anushiik*, and Lottie left feeling proud those tins would be twisted into cones for the jingle dresses at the next powwow.

She began attending tribal meetings, biweekly tobacco ceremonies, and cedar teachings. Lottie started filling Middy's ear with the stuff, and Middy was having none of it. Here she was begging her mom for a helix piercing, and Lottie was going on and on about moon-time and the bleeding lodge. The more she pressed her daughter—*Sacredness!* and *Sisterhood!*—the more Middy tuned her out. Middy's mom had gone soft, spiritual. Sentiment had got to her. She hadn't hollered out the apartment window onto Market Street, like a hellcat in heat, in weeks. The shift in temperament kept Middy and kid brother guessing.

And so when Lottie hung up from Ruthie one smothering afternoon—one so hot the authorities had warned the elderly to stay inside due to the heat index— she turned to Middy and said, "You're going to spend the weekend with your Aunt Ruth in the hills."

"What?" Middy said. "I thought you said the land is poison up there. That they dump sludge and shit."

"It is, they do," her mom quickly conceded, "but one weekend isn't going to send you to the cancer ward."

"*Mom!*" Middy whined. Kid brother cracked up.

"It'll give you a chance to reconnect with your cousin Val."

"Mom!—really now. Who?"

"Stop, Middy. Valerie. She's only a year older than you are. She came to Christmas once. You can hang with her."

"I haven't seen her in years."

"Get reacquainted."

Middy cried foul, saying the arrangement was really about her clearing away her children so she could shack up with her new Bolivian beau in a motel outside Sandy Hook.

"Don't be absurd," Lottie said, though she did little to conceal the fact that's what, for the most part, it *was* about.

"I've been getting in touch with my heritage," Lottie tried, "and so you should too. It's your heritage, too. We share these ancestors."

"Spare me, Mom." Lottie's body slinked and shifted weight in expressions of teeming anger. But her mother prattled on about all this indigenousness—on the changing bodies of young girls; vision quests and the birth of a New Woman; something about sea sponges; clay bowls of cornmeal.

"You know what you sound like?" Middy said. "You sound like how the saleslady at Native Art in Willowbrook Mall looks."

With that, the spirituality evaporated and Middy's mom regressed to full-blown bitch mother.

"You're going, kid. Pack your shit and tell your brother."

Most worrisome for Middy was the tick situation. She'd never seen a tick live and in person but had read a story in the newspaper about them. The weak winter, it said, would mean an uptick in ticks. She read to tuck her pants in her socks, but that was useless advice as she was sitting shotgun in her mom's Hyundai Elantra in booty shorts and jellies. Still, she was excessive with the *Off!* spray, producing a misty cloud in the front seat of the car that made kid brother gag. And, she figured, look at the name: so direct and with an exclamation point to boot. That's smart and effective branding—it would do the trick, for sure. Serious business that bug spray. Lethal.

"Easy with that shit, Middy."

"You're the one making me go into the wilderness, putting my life in danger."

"Your brother's eyes are watering." That was what the boyfriend said. He was in the backseat with kid brother playing travel Connect Four to distract him from the windows. Kid brother got carsick on highways. Middy's mom neglected to restock on Dramamine. She, apparently, preferred to pull over and have him ralph on the roadside.

Well DEETed up, chemicalized from crown to calluses, Middy tried to rest easy. She had her feet on the dash and watched out the window as industry turned to woods.

"They call that dark noise," her mom said.

"Who calls what what?"

"Growing up," Lottie said, "we called the woods dark noise."

"That's stupid," Middy said, watching the trunks of trees pass silently in a green-brown-black blur.

They passed Ringwood State Park, a so-long to civilization proper, and began winding uphill on roads that weren't roads. The radio went weird. Bolivian boyfriend—Middy refused to call him by his name— reached from the backseat and clicked off the dial. He brushed against Middy while doing so, so she *ugh*-ed accordingly.

What she saw out her window was primitive, poorlike. She got worried about more than ticks then. It was all so Appalachian and also getting darker even though, Middy thought, they weren't close to dusk. She suddenly didn't trust the digital numbers on the dash.

"We know people who live here?" she said.

"Yes," her mom answered, "family closer than you even know."

"Strange," Middy said.

It was well and dark when they pulled up to, from what Middy could see, a semi-circle of hovels in a holler. Like a campsite, less a lantern and a s'more station.

Lottie didn't even close her car door as she shoved Middy and kid brother into the welcoming arms of Aunt Ruth.

"Be good," Lottie said, waving.

Bolivian boyfriend hopped from the backseat to the front, not bothering to introduce himself to the extended family.

Val came skipping down a desire path littered with grayed briquettes and empty plastic milk jugs. She was a big girl with her hair pulled back in a tight bun. Short, wet hairs squiggled down from her scalp. Middy immediately thought her cousin must experience nothing short of torture at school. Relentless fat jokes. And, for the record, she had no recollection of ever meeting her before.

"Here comes your cousin!" Ruthie said, forcing the enthusiasm.

"What's that?"

Middy pointed to what looked like a goldfish in a Ziploc. Val was swinging it at her side.

"Oh? This? This thing?" Val held it up to her eyeball and peered into it like she had to remind herself. "This thing is my granmommy's tooth."

It didn't float, but it did when Val bounced the Ziploc. The yellowed tooth was definitely like a goldfish, Middy decided.

"Why do you have it?"

"Why not?"

Val wound up and launched the bag of water and tooth into the ruckus of a lean-to.

"I'll leave you girls to play," Ruthie said. She ushered kid brother off to a crowd of other relatives (Middy guessed they were relatives, anyway), and he wasn't seen again for the remainder of the weekend.

Middy shadowed Val through the woods, following a trail that barely was. She had to swipe branches out of her way and stomp over weed sprouts. Her jellies weren't cut out for it. Val, for her part, wore rugged and unrecognizable hiking boots (they were mud-caked and "talking"—what the kids in New Roberto Clemente said if your shoe soles were flapping loose). She had her t-shirt rolled up and knotted to just below her breasts, baring a frown of belly fat.

"You don't worry about ticks?"

"*Dicks?*" Val whispered.

"You ever gotten a tick bite?"

"I get 'em all the time," Val said. She started her fingers searching over her thick legs. "It's nothing."

Middy imagined engorged critters hanging off Val's thighs and ankles like skin tags. She imagined the blood suck and body expansion until each tick looked like a canvas canteen case.

"Are we gonna be gone long?" Middy asked. She was a shook city girl feeling vulnerable as ever in all that dark noise.

"You ask too many questions," Val said. And that shut Middy up.

She wanted to know where the chiefs were, the elders, the jingle dresses jingling and shimmering in the fairground floodlights or bonfire flames. Where was all her mom had been raving about? Where were the sights that justified her mother's cultural resurgence? Beads? Feathers? Rawhide? *What makes the red man red?* Middy hummed quietly.

All Middy saw was darkness now, and next-level poverty just before. Not Paterson, WIC grocery shopping poorness. But something like those Dorothea Lange photos that appeared on the glossy middle pages of her history textbook.

"How much farther?"

"Just through here," Val said. The woods opened up on the yard of a well-to-do house, though Middy hesitated to say mansion.

Still, there was an inground swimming pool. It was nearly empty, though. It was like someone had tried, tried *really* hard, but couldn't make it so their money showed through in this holler. They'd given up, left the pool to the mosquitoes and frogs.

Val climbed the stairs down into the shallow end. Her boots kicked at clumps of dried leaves and fallen branches.

"C'mon, girlie girl," she said to Middy. "Grab that fish net on your way."

Val picked up a skimmer off the floor of the shallow end, and Middy caught up to her with the fish net. They were armed. For what, Middy didn't know.

The floor of the pool sloped down to greater depths, and soon Middy couldn't see over the edge. If it were full, she'd be submerged.

With the skimmer at her hip, Val kneeled down before the mucky, black water at the deep end. Middy could smell the stink of it, and only the bleachy whiteness of the pool's walls kept her from being scared shitless.

"Hold the net steady over here," Val said. She smacked her hip, which seemed even meatier while squatting.

She glided the skimmer along the surface of the shallow water, gathering mostly algae. Only when water started splashing did Middy realize Val was scooping up frogs. It startled her, the spritzing of bacteria-laden water—brain-eating amoebas, paramecium, what have you.

"Take these," Val told her. "Take these up in the net."

The frogs—small, thin things Middy couldn't recognize from children's books and cartoons—flopped in the knotty nylon of the fish net. Searching legs poked through its holes.

Val threw the skimmer to the side—hollow aluminum clanging, empty pool echoing. She strong-armed the fish net away from Middy and scampered up the slope of the pool bottom and up the stairs.

"C'mon now," Val whisper-yelled. "C'mon, c'mon. Climb, climb, climb!"

She was booking it. Middy could keep up easily if it weren't for the bracken ferns and spindly branches blocking the trail Val was blazing. It was difficult to maintain her footing (those jellies—*never again*), and Val's boots were hitting hard, her stride impressive, athletic even.

Eventually the woods opened up on a meadow, and the moonlight provided ample light.

"There," Val told Middy. "That boulder there."

It was flat on its face—smooth rock. Val untwisted the fish net, drove her hand in, and pulled out a frog by its hind legs. She whipped it against the rock.

"Take one," Val said. "Have at it."

But Middy stood back, a safe distance, and watched. She watched as Val began to grunt a little and wind her arm like a softball pitcher. She used her whole body. Middy didn't know if it was blood and guts or just wetness leaving marks on the rock. There wasn't a whole lot of what she'd consider croaking. Some frogs survived, scampering into tall grasses. Others, she assumed from the thuds at the base of the rock, did not.

Back at the house, Middy's uncle—whose name, she realized, she still didn't know—was being fireman-carried through the Bilco doors from the basement. When his drinking buddies got him to the picnic table, he proceeded to puke into a sheetrock bucket.

"We hang out in the basement a lot," Val said. "It stays cool down there in the summer."

Middy's uncle's skin was weathered but his eyes were watery, crying. His cargo shorts were hiked high up on his thighs. Keloid scars wormed along his legs.

"My dad tripped holding a chainsaw," Val said proudly. "Doctors said he missed his femoral artery by an inch—by *this* much," she pinched.

Disoriented and dog-tired, that's how Middy felt. Val had run her ragged through the woods, and now she was talking her ear off. It was like she was catching her up on everything she'd been missing out on—a lifetime's worth.

"Let me show you how we used to stay cool."

"Can we go inside? I'm beat," Middy said.

"It's not far like the pool," Val told her. "Really. It's right over the hill there." She was pointing into darkness.

True, it wasn't far. It was a gaping mine adit that blew breaths of crisp air from deep in the earth. Subterranean coolness. Middy opened her mouth to it like a tonic. Val got closer to the actual entrance, climbing over cinderblocks and rocks and debris. Middy stayed back, not wanting to chance it. Nothing would say successful summer outing like a misplaced step and a gut impaled by rusty rebar.

"That's where they dump paint sludge and everything else," Val shouted at Middy. "And so that's why we can't sit here anymore. It's in our dirt and water, too," she added, shrugging. "The sludge."

"What do you mean?"

"What do you mean what do I mean?" Val started back to where Middy was standing, level ground. "You're not so smart, are you?"

"Who dumps paint sludge in there?"

"Trucks come and dump their loads into the mines. My dad says it's a cheap way to do it. Just dump it on us."

Middy began walking back toward the house again. She felt emboldened seeing Val following. She was the leader, for once. It'd been hours since she was in her mom's Hyundai.

"It kills us, I guess." Val's voice hit her from behind—a wilderness voice, a keening banshee.

"Well yeah," Middy said. She left off the *duh*.

That day unraveled into the next. There didn't seem to be a next day, just one instant after another. Especially since Middy barely slept. The air mattress deflated through the night, and she feared ticks crawling over her and into her being so close to the ground. She ended up on the couch, which was no better.

It wasn't even nine in the morning when Aunt Ruthie told Middy and Val they weren't doing diddlysquat. She'd hear the same if she were home.

What's with adults so concerned with productivity, she thought. Slave drivers, the lot of 'em.

Breakfast was eaten in the living room on a shared tray table. Both girls fletcherized their food, and so the meal took forever.

The man Middy took at everyone's word as her uncle was near sober now, and his eyes blinked rapidly, continuously, like he was flushing particulate from them without the help of water. He not so much watched television as clicked through the channels, often stopping on commercials. He chugged a mug of lukewarm coffee and knocked it against his knee to a beat. Middy watched his keloids.

"You heard those trucks last night, Middy?"

She was startled he even knew her name.

"Trucks?"

"The dump trucks. Dumping their slime in the mines. Val, you tell her?"

"I told her. She's not a good listener."

"I heard what you said, Val." Middy said it with a tone she'd typically reserved for her mom. "And I heard the trucks, too."

The trucks had a low grumble, grinding gears like shrieks. Middy's head filled with all the spooky associations of forest lore, and she had fallen in and out of sleep with those thoughts keeping her company.

"Fucking bastards," her uncle said.

The cousins stood side-by-side at the bathroom sink with Val hogging much of the counter and mirror space. She bodied Middy to the side.

Middy forgot to pack a toothbrush, so she used her pointer finger. The sulfur water spilling from the sink stunk. It was sickening, nearly gagging Middy. Val died at this, frothing at the corners of her mouth in laughter.

"You're ridiculous," she said, but it was garbled.

Outside, Middy sniffed at her fingers.

They swam in a smaller lake off Cupsaw Lake. Middy called it a pond and Val set her straight. But it was the muck—the viscid, intestines-like grunge—on the bottom of the lake that made Middy say pond. She thought the lily pads made it so as well.

She thought about bloodied frogs, about toxic sludge. And the small lake also made Middy think about indigenous life.

"Did you go to that powwow?" Middy asked.

"What powwow?"

"My mom went to a powwow up here a while ago."

"Oh. Yeah," Val said. "I was there, but I don't really do the native shit unless I'm forced to. Do you?"

"Nah, we don't fuck with that sort of shit. Just my mom," Middy said, feeling the need to up her daily curse count to match Val's garbage heap of a mouth.

Absent canoe rides, calumets, beadwork and feathers, Middy's visit to her native kin in the hills wasn't what she expected.

Take *calumet*, for instance. She'd learned that word for peace pipe from school. New Roberto Clemente was, at least, on-point with field trips. Her fifth grade class traveled west to Byram Township in a green school bus (it was a yellow school bus before it was used to transport prisoners; then it was back to transporting the kiddies, but the coat of green paint—stenciled DOC on the sides—and mesh on the windows remained). Waterloo Village recreated a Lenape village. Middy saw huts made of tree bark and saplings, a long house, animal pelts stretched between branches for curing. After lunch at wooden picnic tables with inchworms walking the lumber between lunch boxes, their guide brought out a calumet, a peace pipe, she said. Each kid passed it around the circle, and only Wilberto broke the rules by putting it to his lips.

"This is pretty much it," Val said. She splashed her arm against the surface of the water. She flicked at it with her chubby fingers.

"Why's my mom always talking about getting in touch with her cultural heritage and shit like that then?"

"I mean, we do the powwows in fall and spring," she said. "But that's like, you know, we go to church on Christmas and Easter, too. That sort of thing."

So much for the sacred mumbo-jumbo Middy's mom had been spewing for months.

"Maybe your mom talks to mine about those things," Val said. "Maybe they discuss chasing buffalo off cliffs together."

Maybe her mom was kneeling on a hotel pillow right

now, Middy thought. Maybe she was blowing her Bolivian boyfriend. Maybe he was going to come on her face.

Dragonflies flirted with the surface of the water. Middy tracked their twinkling iridescence. Val heaved toward the shoreline.

"Let's go."

"Why now?"

There was an older man with overalls entering the water some yards off: grizzled beard with patches of white. The color powdered his lips. His denim went dark as he got deeper into the lake. He was making for the girls, his hands in the air in an expression of innocence or a reluctance to get them wet.

"That's Chauncey," Val said. "Nothing but trouble. And my mom doesn't let us near him."

They walked so much—woods, trails or not—and Middy was without bug spray. She coated her calves and ankles in hand cream, but it didn't do much good. Mosquito bites spread to full-blown welts. She scratched at them and they bled.

"Leave it alone, for fuck's sake," Val told her.

Val kept playing the role of tour guide. In the crooks of trees, tent caterpillars crawled up the interior white walls of their nests. Middy recoiled.

"I call those Dead Woman's Vagina," Val said.

In a spinney of chokecherry trees, Val pointed to the black-knot fungus growing on the branches. The galls were hardened into charred-looking tumors. Val reached and peeled them away from bark.

"We throw these at strangers," she said. "People come into our area to harass us? We unload these on them. We call it Dookie Attacks."

"Who comes into your area to harass you guys?"

"Private school kids, local news people. You'd be surprised."

Val chucked the black gall ahead of her, aiming at nothing.

"You should wash your hands after holding that," Middy said.

"You're a priss."

The last leg of their journey cut through a cemetery. Val called it *the colored folk burial plot*. "That's what it says in books and shit," she said.

Tombstones were skinny, slate slabs—uneven tops and sides. They weren't very ornamental, just flat rock chiseled at until names and numbers were adequately visible. Age had made the epitaphs, by and large, unreadable. A poetic line here, a description of kinship there. They'd all been uprooted and tilted by mining, sunken deeper in some cases, too.

It would be useless work to straighten the tombstones. This was a forgotten parcel of land. There were no spirits there, and so no eeriness.

They made it back for dinner—hotdogs with skins that really snapped, homegrown slaw, and pickle chips as an official side. And then it was darkness, and then it was drunkenness.

The adults absconded into the basement, the open Bilco doors emitting a shaft of lantern light that looked as if it was the hatch entrance to a flying saucer.

Time warp. Wormhole. Black hole. Multiverse. Fallout shelter. Historical hiccup.

Someone, probably Middy's uncle, pitched empties up the concrete stairwell. Cans upon caved-in cans littered the dirt yard. It was a safe bet nobody'd be bagging those until morning.

"Let's walk," Val told her. They were sitting on the picnic table, elevated for safety from critters. Middy closed in on herself, hugging her torso. She massaged her kneecaps. Val, meanwhile, sat like a hunter at rest might, with legs spread and gesticulations that dominated the space around her.

A bug zapper hanging from a nearby tree discharged volts into the Mothra of all moths.

"More walking?" Middy said, almost angry. She

looked through the window on her aunt's house and saw the illumination from the TV. She knew kid brother was in there, enduring the final hours of the weekend with cartoons.

"What else are we gonna do?" Val said. She hopped off the picnic table and the lumber creaked. Middy knew her cousin's heft would be breaking it to tinder in time.

She had to stop this, she thought. Her internal ripping on Val came easy, but over the course of their hours together she'd developed a fondness for her companion, her helpmeet, her cousin. This wasn't some friend from school—this was blood. And Val was doing her best with what she had to keep Middy entertained.

"I have to use the bathroom," Middy said, "then we'll go."

"Okay," Val said, lifting herself back onto the picnic table. "Don't fall in."

The bathroom was so narrow Middy's knees almost hit the door. She was bloated from barbecue and wanted to move her bowels before her next walk cramped them.

She focused on a family portrait on the back of the sink. It was in a craft frame made from popsicle sticks and beach shells. Hot glue hairs outlined the shells and smooth pink pebbles, too. Middy considered whether those were really her relatives in the photo. Here she was living with them, essentially strangers. She'd be just as well spending the time in child predator Chauncey's trailer, she thought.

She tried to feel the closeness, and she did to a degree. She felt it with Val, anyway. Not her Aunt Ruthie or drunk uncle, though—she still didn't even know his name. But if her blood was in Val's, and her mom's was in Aunt Ruthie's, then that's a bond to feel for—*right?* The more family you've got the more security? It would figure, at least. It wasn't like her dad. His distance made her feel at sea, and he was only two towns over in Passaic. *He* wasn't native—that was for certain. His people were from Georgia originally. That made her only half of all this. She didn't have to own it in its entirety if she didn't want to. She could joke about it, joyride through the holler in some indeterminate future with friends from school. She could tell those friends the people in this holler—these degenerate hillfolk—had guns, lots of 'em. In a few years when she and her friends were of driving age, she could ride in the backseat, hiding in the darkness of a vehicle at night. She could do what she pleased with this native life. She could take it or leave it or disparage it or pretend it wasn't even there.

Middy followed Val as she cut through the dark. This time Middy stared at the muscles in Val's legs, the mass of her cousin's body. She noticed the sweat running in rivulets down her calves—its wild glistening.

Val was in full possession of her body. The comportment of her limbs was feral, unconstrained. She was in total control of the space she filled, and so the woods bent around her to create an avenue all her own. Middy simply followed.

Middy wasn't like Val. Middy lived life in a box she often visualized as a pine coffin. She'd already learned how to skip out on gym class by telling Coach Dykstra she was on her period. Anything to avoid mountain climbers and crunches and the general embarrassment of physical education.

Val was unburdened. Her clothes were dappled with sweat. Nothing seemed to bother her. Comparatively, Middy felt inessential. Val bounded across a stream, fearlessly, while Middy toed a moss-covered stone bridging the water, put off by its wobble. She had to coax her body to cross the stream, which was not so easily willed and accomplished. Yonder was nothing to Val—she was already there.

They returned to the cemetery.

"Here again?"

"You hate it here, don't you?" Val said.

Middy didn't know if she meant *here* the cemetery or *here* the holler, the woods, the ancestral land, so she didn't answer.

Val slumped down against a tombstone, and Middy did the same. She couldn't make out the engraving, so she assumed it wasn't too blasphemous. She wasn't trying to provoke ghosts and deface graves by pressing her scrawny back to it.

They sat for a moment, stilly, Val finally having shut up. The volume of the wilderness is what's supposed to startle city folk, but Middy was more put off by the heat and swarming insects. She swatted some unknown bug away from her face, its wings shuttering in the starlight.

"You get your period yet?"

Val asked the question without turning her head. They'd both been staring straight into the darkness, into the woods that made for the most mysterious and unmapped hiding-place ever. She pivoted her head to Middy to repeat the question.

"Have you or what?"

"My period? Yeah, of course. You haven't?"

"No, I have. Never said anything about me. I was asking you."

If Middy hadn't just experienced the most un-Indian thirty-six hours of her life, she'd expect this to be the moment when Val started talking about moontimes and the bleeding lodge—all that girl-transition-in-to-woman talk that her mom had tried on her.

"My mom calls it the red road," Val said.

"A girl in my class says Aunt Flo's visiting."

Val laughed louder than was necessary and knocked her head against the tombstone.

"That's funny shit," she said.

"Are you okay? Did you concuss yourself?"

Now they were both laughing, shouldering into each other in convulsions like two strangers slipping on the same patch of ice and struggling to get back up.

"You on it now?"

"On *it*?"

"Your period," Val said with a shove.

"No."

"Me neither," Val said, then pausing. "You know if you come here every weekend or if we lived together we would bleed together."

"Yeah?"

"Yeah. My mom told me it works like that. Is that crazy or what?"

"Crazy," Middy said. "Witchy, almost."

A passenger jet flew overhead, a light on its underside blinking. It brought Middy back to Paterson, to streetlights and traffic signals and the honking horns of jitney buses. Not homesick, though. Not right then. She adjusted her back against the tombstone. The clasp of her bra was digging into her skin.

"You jerk off yet?" Val asked.

All Middy knew of the term was how it was used at New Roberto Clemente. Alvin and Reggie and Mo called each other jerk-offs. And they called Mr. Palmer, the STEM teacher, a jerk-off too. She didn't want to seem too young, too naive—since Val's questions all seemed designed to achieve just that—so she said *Yeah*.

"How'd you do it?"

"Do what? Jerk off?"

"Yes, dummy.

Middy looked left and right as though she were watching for cars.

"I don't know," she said, dismissively.

"You want to know how I do it?"

"Whatever."

"The bathroom tub," Val said with no shortage of pride. She did a sort of wink, a grandpa or uncle wink that tells you he's just hipped you to something, something good. "You put yourself under the faucet and run the water—you'll be done in a few minutes. If you don't feel anything, then you ain't doing it right."

Middy got the impression Val was really enjoying sharing this knowledge, this expertise. It was as though all their time together had been building up to this, as though Val had been holding both hands over her mouth waiting for the opportunity to say what she was saying.

"You want to do it now?"

"What?"

Middy made eye contact with Val and then didn't for some time.

"Jerk off. I can do it for you."

"*Umm*," Middy said, drawing it out into a meditative vibration. The dark noise thrumming.

"It's easier if we were in the bathroom, but I can do it with my hand, too."

Middy hemmed some more, and Val kept talking.

"We're not really cousins, y'know," she said. "Ruthie took me in. My parents died in a car crash when I was a baby." Middy didn't know if that was a joke or what. She thought it was a strange thing to say.

Val kept at her, "What, you sure you're not on your period?"

That got Middy to turn back to her.

"I told you I wasn't," she said with some agitation. She felt like Val was trying to say that Middy hadn't bled yet, which she hadn't.

"Alright, alright," Val said with her hands up in defense.

Middy adjusted against the tombstone. The notches of her spine ached.

"You can do it."

"You sure?" Val asked. "I don't want to make you do something you don't want to. Or if you're scared."

"Do it, okay?"

So Val leaned into Middy and reached her hand over the crotch of her shorts. She rubbed there for a moment before unbuttoning and unzipping the shorts. Her hand slid down the front of Middy's cotton underwear. Middy breathed deeply and slumped further down the tombstone. She closed her eyes and felt her skin shiver like a cold sweat. Her eyelids fluttered and she experienced a series of fleeting thoughts splurting out like polluting fluids. She thought of engorged ticks, of her mother and the Bolivian boyfriend, of zombie hands pushing through the dirt like flower bulbs budding to grab at her. She thought about Val's hand and what it was doing. How the fingertips moved through the fogbank of curly hairs there, triangled and tufted. And when she thought of that, she thought of Little Miss Muffet sitting on her tuffet. She opened her eyes and watched the sky for passenger jets before staring straight ahead into all the dark noise.

"She got too much sun," Bolivian boyfriend said.

He was driving the Hyundai Elantra now. Her mom was in the backseat with kid brother, her body seemingly suspended by the seat belt and her head tilted back like all the ligaments had given out. The skin on her face was darkened but lighter around the eyes from her sunglasses. Hair all beach-blown. She looked like a madwoman.

Middy was fantasizing about a car crash—just a sudden turn of the wheel and collision with a guardrail. Her mom would never forgive Bolivian boyfriend, and that would solve the problem of his too frequent presence in their apartment. No more Lottie blowjobs for him.

"Did you have fun with your cousin?" he asked.

Odds were good this was the only direct question Bolivian boyfriend had ever asked her. It startled her from her window gazing bloody, metal-crushing reverie. She looked at him—scanned him up and down. A real sizing up. He was driving with his knees pressed to the bottom of the steering wheel to free his hands for the peeling of an orange. The fruit looked so small in his hands, and then Middy realized it was a clementine. He dug a creepily long thumbnail into the rind to start it, and he deftly removed the entire rind in one piece. He lowered the window to toss it out, and Middy turned around to watch it tumble along the highway shoulder.

"I guess," she answered. She hadn't even seen Val that morning. She apparently got up early to go ATVing with her dad. Middy knew there was no delaying when the Elantra pulled into the holler. Her mom hurried her into the car, waving so long and thank you to Aunt Ruthie. There was no goodbye from Val. Val might as well have never been.

"She nice or a smart ass like you?"

He turned to her with three clementine segments shoved into his mouth, a juicy smile gushing all that was in there. He delicately removed the white strings from the segments in his hand and loosed them from his fingers onto the floor mat. Middy chose to ignore his question and switch the subject.

"Do you believe in Indians?"

The question surprised her as much as it did Bolivian boyfriend.

"Do I *what*?"

"That's not what I meant. I mean have you ever seen an Indian? A Native American."

A line of spittle mixed with juice dribbled down his chin and disappeared into his goatee. He wiped at it, roughly, with his knuckles and back of his hand.

"Uh, I can't say for sure."

"Do you think those people you just picked me up from are natives?"

"Ohhhh," Bolivian boyfriend said, still chewing. "You're talking about all this Indian bullshit your momma's gotten into."

"They're my family," Middy said.

"Yeah, don't I know it?" He made an exhausted face, like he was so over hearing about it. Middy felt he hadn't been around long enough to have a claim to that sort of reaction, though. "Your mom is needing something," he said.

"What's that supposed to mean?"

He held up a finger and pursed his lips together. A slimy, stringy seed dropped into his upturned palm. It was mangled, so he must have bit down on it. He placed it into the console cupholder where it mingled with crusty pennies, a pen cap, and balled-up gum wrappers. He took a quick glance in the rearview mirror, wiped his hands on his pants, and placed them back on the steering wheel.

"Your mom is trying to connect with people," he said. "She feels the need for human connection, y'know? She's reconnecting with her family, for better or worse. I'm not too sure about them."

"What do you mean you're not too sure about them? What about them?"

"I'm just saying—and I told her this—I wouldn't be dropping you kids off with them for a weekend in the woods if you were mine."

"You told her that?"

"Yeah I told her that. Shit, we argued for the entire drive down the shore."

Middy stared at him, then out the window beyond him, and thought of him and her mom arguing side-by-side in the front seat of the car just as she was sitting side-by-side with him right now.

"Why wouldn't you drop us off with them?"

Bolivian boyfriend shook his head.

"It's not important. Clearly you guys did fine. You survived. You got to know your cousin. My point wasn't that. My point was to tell you your mom is desperate for connections right now. That's how we hooked up. We were both in a down, low, shitty place, and we commiserated and got along. She wants to connect with you better, you know. You should give her the time of day."

"Don't tell me how to get along with my mom," Middy snapped.

"I won't," he said.

Middy turned to look out her window again. She wanted to stare into dark noise, but all she saw now were factory smokestacks and billboards. They were almost home, and she heard her mom stirring awake in the backseat. Middy swung her feet up onto the dash and caressed her legs up and down, checking for ticks. Her mom started to say something to her, but Middy closed her eyes like she couldn't be bothered with anything anytime soon, especially if it was coming from her mother.

A Posthumous Existence

WHAT HE WANTED WAS for his parents to be dead. Mother and father both. You could lace it with tragic details, sure, or have them expire with a wimpy whimper. Whichever. Once they were gone, so would he be. What was Holmdel anyway? Home of Bell Labs? Big whoop. The thing is, he needed to be orphaned if he was going to be a serious artist. He'd need to end up in the Pacific Northwest—Puget Sound or somewhere. He needed to shuck this New Jersey husk. He'd need to figure out how to work a camera, a real one, not the throwaway ones his mom used at his graduation ceremony. Or if he couldn't learn exposure time and all that, he could buy the throwaway cameras from Rite

Aids across the rotten-fruited plains and masturbate on the photos. People did that, you know. Rich people lined up to see it. He didn't want to go that way, but he kept it stored upstairs as a point to make to people who doubted him.

Holmdel was lilywhite, boring enough to make him huff chlorofluorocarbons for kicks, for ruthless fun. That's the sort of place it was. Would the Pacific Northwest be any different? Probably not. He met a guy from Montana who told him Coeur d'Alene was full of Aryan Nation thin-pricks. No worries, he thought. He can just pass over Idaho like cloud cover. The same Montana guy told him there was a ferry you could catch from Washington to Alaska—that you could pitch your tent and camp right on the deck. He could do that, he thought. Just as soon as his mother was stricken with some carcinoma.

He walked around the ring road of Bell Labs on days he wouldn't sweat or shiver to death. The whole while he felt he was leading a posthumous existence, like he'd read Keats put down into a letter. Then he read the Keats letter. He needed the authentic experience of it. Not to say he was coughing up blood into a hanky, but he was over *this*. "This" was best expressed with his arms outstretched, his hands rotating rapidly at the wrists. For godsakes, he was a person who read

Keats! Bell Labs was covered in mirrored glass so that it reflected the trees and culvert ponds and shrubbery and open fields surrounding it. If the lighting was right, and your angle was right, it would vanish. It reminded him of when David Copperfield made a Learjet disappear on a primetime TV special. Copperfield had people surround the plane, blindfolded—everyone holding hands. This was to help sell the trick. But it made the spectacle seem so much more cultish.

Always with a book, for he thought any serious artist should always be with a book, he had a fourth printing of Gary Snyder's *The Back Country*. He found it in a bookstore, believe it or not. He cherished it. The spine was Scotch-taped decades ago, and that handiwork was yellow and peeling. He liked walking the ring road and parking lots around Bell Labs while holding that Snyder collection in front of his face, blocking out the sun. He'd read a poem halfway, return to its start, and slog through it again. You had to read poems more than once, he knew. What a time-waster. He'd close the book, his finger keeping his page, and contemplate the words. The book was broken up into sections, each marked with an ink-wash enzō circle. The cover was a ground's-eye view of old-growth trees, a burst in the canopy. Snyder called nature "green shit," and he thought that was lovely. But his mind would wander.

He was very much about wandering. *Wanderlust.* That was a word he kept close. He thought about Snyder as Japhy Ryder in *Dharma Bums* having spiritual threesomes on the cabin carpet. He thought about the Nobel laureates turning over numbers and conducting experiments in Bell Labs. The cell phone was birthed there. He knew that.

He wanted to take double-exposure photos on the Canon AE-1 he bought off eBay. He knew, in theory, authenticity was bullshit. He'd read the books on that. But, still, he felt he needed to document his happening on actual, physical, tangible, flammable film. In theory he knew how—it was simple, even for him, a kid who couldn't comprehend manuals or tackle anything even remotely technical. All he had to do was click the rewind button, wind the lever, and fake the film advancing. He wanted to take photos of people's faces superimposed over nature: hillsides and riptides and cloudscapes. He could do that so much better out West, he knew. Bluffs, plateaus, open skies, et al. But he needed film. And he needed the will to go. Were his parents casket-bound yet?

He wanted it just so, so that he had nothing to lose. Nothing to lose except a billfold with damp, wrinkly ones in it and a Timex on his wrist. And he wanted to lose those—either on public transit or while sleeping in a warehouse-cum-commune. He longed to get robbed by someone he loved, someone he trusted. Betrayal is something worth experiencing, at least once. It would give him something to talk about with some stranger at an indeterminate point in the future. Maybe, just maybe, he could get a thumping in a boxcar. That would be romantic—an ass-beating with snapshots of America clicking by.

He hated his mom's habit of keeping her bed pillow on the sofa. Awful enough the sofa was covered in a flannel sheet, which would always pull loose and gather at the cushion seams, collecting crumbs and such. The bed pillow had no business there. It told him his mom would be loafing for the daylong. He'd take scabies and cold showers over having to see her on that sofa, fetal, through *Maury*, *Jenny Jones*, *Ricki Lake*, *Sally Jesse*, and soaps. He'd never want to rest his head on her pillow, but it was always there—flattened, inviting. He'd settle in and watch infomercials late at night, early morning.

The best was the *Summer of Love* box set. The infomercial was hosted by an aging, but still childishly handsome, Davy Jones. His introductions and commentary were delivered from a set designed to invoke nostalgia for the period. Colorful construction paper flowers and peace signs everywhere. Uncomfortable, golden-brown basement furniture. Walls with wood paneling. Haight-Ashbury was commercialized now, he'd heard. Gone were the psych-rock bands living free lovingly together in third-floor apartments. San Francisco was too far south for him, anyway. He was the deadest of dead-set on the Pacific Northwest. He wanted the Cascades and anarchist collectives. He wasn't gonna be wooed by *Come on people now, smile on your brother* or wearing flowers in your hair. He didn't want to grow his beard in dense tangles and wear complicated, flowing long-sleeve shirts that made him look like a guru. Zonked out of his mind and meandering the doors of perception? Nah, he wasn't about it. He knew there wasn't, eternally, gentle people there. He'd seen enough documentaries to know there were more murders, death cults, and toddlers on acid trips to take San Francisco out of the running.

Once he got to Portland, or Seattle, or Eugene, or Aberdeen, or Olympia he could start writing. He'd be adequately weathered and sufficiently straggly. He'd look the part. He'd fit right in. He might even purchase a Corona typewriter at a second-hand store. He'd be brazen and approach likeminded people on the street. He'd be hipped to the underground venues. He'd offer up hours at the food co-op. He'd hang out in studios at college radio stations and steal the promo CDs with the barcodes punched out.

He'd begin anew. He knew his father never went to Yale. He knew his mother was no hospital CEO. He knew she never worked as a legislative aid to Walter Mondale. He knew he'd never sailed or skied. He would never get a Guggenheim or Whiting or Pulitzer. His prizes were all consolation ones, he knew. He'd never have to refer to a time when he was "going to school in New Haven" as a way to shamefacedly avoid saying "Yale." He wouldn't have to take joy in admitting that shame, because admitting that shame would be cute. He wasn't a descendant of colonial settlers with the paperwork to prove it. His great-grandfather didn't own half the real estate in Deadwood. He had no private schooling. He wouldn't be burdened with telling anybody in the Pacific Northwest any of this. What a freedom. What a liberating, orgasmic feeling. Thank god his parents were poor, were dead. He'd take such pleasure in telling everyone so. All he had to do was get started.

If it was wrong to have fantasies then what was the point of consciousness? His number one, primo fantasy concerned blowing up Bell Labs. He'd just turned twelve when Timothy McVeigh drove his Ryder rental truck into the Murrah building in Oklahoma City. Did ammonium nitrate rattle? Would he have to brake at railroad crossings? Would he have to do an interview on *60 Minutes* to explain his ideology? Would they edit the footage so that he was intercut with the family members of his victims, coldly calling for his lethal injection with the stoicism family members of atrocity victims are known for? Would they schedule interviews with his parents, set up the cameras and umbrella lighting in his childhood bedroom? Would the producer of the piece tell his mother to make her bed pillow disappear from the sofa? Would his father cry? None of it would matter. His parents would be dead and soon so would he.

Joseph Rathgeber is from New Jersey. He has received fellowships from the New Jersey State Council on the Arts and the National Endowment for the Arts. He has previously published a novel, *Mixedbloods*, two poetry collections, *MJ* and *Soft Money*, and a short story collection, *The Abridged Autobiography of Yousef R.* He doesn't believe in author photos.

Fomite

More story collections from Fomite...

MaryEllen Beveridge — *After the Hunger*
MaryEllen Beveridge — *Permeable Boundaries*
Jay Boyer — *Flight*
L. M Brown — *Treading the Uneven Road*
L. M Brown — *Were We Awake*
Michael Cocchiarale — *Here Is Ware*
Michael Cocchiarale — *Still Time*
Neil Connelly — *In the Wake of Our Vows*
Catherine Zobal Dent — *Unfinished Stories of Girls*
Zdravka Evtimova —*Carts and Other Stories*
John Michael Flynn — *Off to the Next Wherever*
Derek Furr — *Semitones*
Derek Furr — *Suite for Three Voices*
Elizabeth Genovise — *Where There Are Two or More*
Andrei Guriuanu — *Body of Work*
Zeke Jarvis — *In A Family Way*
Arya Jenkins — *Blue Songs in an Open Key*
Bobby Johnston — *The Saint I Ain't*
Jan English Leary — *Skating on the Vertical*
Julia MacDonnell— *The Topography of Hidden Stories*
Marjorie Maddox — *What She Was Saying*
William Marquess — *Badtime Stories*
William Marquess — *Because Because Because Because Because*
William Marquess — *Boom-shacka-lacka*
William Marquess — *Things I Want You to Do*
Gary Miller — *Museum of the Americas*
Jennifer Anne Moses — *Visiting Hours*
Martin Ott — *Interrogations*
George Ovitt — *The Showcase*

Christopher Peterson — *Amoebic Simulacra*
Christopher Peterson — *Scratch the Itchy Teeth*
Charles Phillips — *Dead South*
Jack Pulaski — *Love's Labours*
Charles Rafferty — *Saturday Night at Magellan's*
Joseph Rathgeber — *Bad Days on the Batso*